KILL-BOX

When Private Eye Steve Ericson is asked by Dolly to keep an eye on her cheating husband Michael aboard the overnight Chicago-to-New York Express, it seems like a routine gig. But by the time the train rolls into Grand Central, the case has already gone off the rails: Michael is dead, causes unknown. Steve knows something is off-beat; anyone in the carriages could be involved — atomic scientists and beautiful women included. With the cops already eyeballing Dolly, Steve must clear her name — which wasn't all that untarnished to begin with . . .

LAWRENCE LARIAR

KILL-BOX

Complete and Unabridged

LINFORD
Leicester

First published in Great Britain

First Linford Edition
published 2020

A catalogue record for this book is available
from the British Library.

ISBN 978–1–4448–4403–0

Published by
F. A. Thorpe (Publishing)
Anstey, Leicestershire

Set by Words & Graphics Ltd.
Anstey, Leicestershire
Printed and bound in Great Britain by
T. J. International Ltd., Padstow, Cornwall

This book is printed on acid-free paper

The author wishes to make grateful acknowledgement to John W. Campbell, Jr., Science Editor of Street and Smith, Inc., for the technical advice, essential to the story, pertaining to nuclear physics.

1

The woman in the green suit sat at the far end of the bar, framed against the small street window of Harry's Five Lights Bar. She was a static silhouette against the gray light of Chicago in the street beyond her. She perched on her stool in the dainty pose all women must assume while sipping liquor from a high stool. She leaned on both elbows and talked to Harry. Her legs were crossed so that I could see them and enjoy the interesting highlights on her nylons. She wore small red shoes, decorated with silk bows and studded with brass nails around the toe.

After a while I tired of her dimpled knees and tapped my empty glass on the bar and Harry heard me and came over.

He filled it with another highball and said: 'I'll be with you in a few shakes, Steve. Don't go 'way.'

He walked back to the woman and folded his big hands on his chest and just stood there listening to her, nodding his head occasionally and showing her his broad and tolerant smile. She was drinking a cocktail as she talked, in short nervous gulps. Her little mouth kept moving in a quick monologue but her eyes held him in a steady and purposeful stare. And Harry stood there nodding his head and smiling at her with his empty blue eyes.

After a while he leaned toward her on one elbow and she listened and turned her head to follow his finger. She looked at me. I caught Harry's slow wink. He said a few more words to her and she shrugged and got off the stool and walked to a booth. She walked with a nice movement. She had the high-heeled grace of a chorus girl. And the hips to go with it.

Harry came down to my end of the bar. Without turning his head in her direction he picked up a glass, polished it and said: 'Something for you, Steve. You like it?'

I said, 'I'm not in the mood for it, Harry.'

Harry laughed in his quiet way. 'Don't be a slob, Steve. The little lady has troubles. She wants to meet you.'

'I can live without her. Is she lit?'

'She only had four Manhattans. That ain't much for her.'

'You know her?'

'She's been in before. A good customer.'

'Dough?'

Harry sighed. 'What do you want, a Dun and Bradstreet rating? You're a detective. That hunk of fur on her shoulders is worth more than my furniture and fixtures.'

I turned my head so that I could see her in the long mirror behind the bar. In the booth, she was smoking a cigarette. She held it in her mouth, man style. Her well-polished fingernails were tapping a quick rhythm on Harry's checkered tablecloth.

I said, 'What's bothering her?'

Harry placed the polished glass on the counter under the mirror with a delicate gesture. 'She didn't say because I didn't ask her. A bartender don't fiddle with lady customers that way.'

I put a five-dollar bill on the bar and Harry covered it with his big hand. He said, 'I'll take the fin because I figure you'll make a deal with her. It's a nice pitch for you, Steve. You waltz in here for a few quick ones and right away pick up a customer. That don't happen every day to a private eye.'

I left him and walked over to her booth and when she waved me to a seat I sat down.

She smiled a nervous smile, quick and meaningless. Without taking the cigarette out of her mouth she said, 'What were you drinking, Mr. Ericson?'

'I've had enough, thanks. How about you?'

'I need another Manhattan. I've only just begun.'

I turned to Harry and he nodded at me from behind the bar. I saw him lift the makings of her drink. He worked quickly, mixed it and then came over and put it down near her. She fumbled with her purse but Harry held up a hand and smiled his professional smile and said,

'That one's on the house. Let's keep it friendly.'

Up close, she had a pert nose, wide cold eyes, a small and petulant mouth and dark hair, parted in the middle. A delicate yet penetrating scent floated around her and fought a losing fight with the fragrances from Harry's kitchen.

She studied her drink. 'Harry tells me that you're a detective on the way to New York. Is that true?'

'Harry never lies.'

She looked up at me for a fleeting glance and her eyes were full of worry. 'I suppose this is a queer way to hire a detective, isn't it?'

'I wouldn't know. I've never hired one.'

I let the silence grow around us. She took the cigarette out of her mouth and held it over the ashtray. She studied the end of it, tapped it nervously against the tray, turned it in her fingers and then ground it out. Her hand was trembling when she toyed with the stem of the cocktail glass.

She said, 'Can you take the train for New York tonight?'

'I can take a flying leap for the moon if you give me a reason and an expense account. What's doing in New York?'

She tried for a smile, but didn't quite make it. She was losing control, slowly but surely. I pulled out my little black book and began to ask the routine questions. Her name was Mrs. Dolly DePereyra. She was leaving for New York with her husband. They lived on Park Avenue.

I said, 'What do you want me to do?'

Without looking up, she answered, 'I want you to watch my husband.'

I coughed hard to avoid laughing. It was the same old pitch, complete with hot and cold running jealousy. 'What's the matter with your husband?'

Her hands weren't holding themselves well. They were mutilating a lace handkerchief.

'I don't blame you for laughing,' she said softly. 'You probably see lots of cases like me, women who don't trust their husbands. But I can't stand it any longer. It's been going on for years with us. I've tried — I've fought against it, but it's no

6

use. Tonight I decided that I'd do something about it. When I walked in here and began to talk to Harry I must have — '

'I didn't mean to laugh, Mrs. DePereyra,' I said soberly. 'And it won't help any to let out your emotional stops. Tailing husbands is routine for me. Tell me, what does he look like?'

She made a great show of putting the brakes on. She showed me a photograph of her husband, a classic profile topped with blond and curling locks. I studied the picture and studied her, beyond the edge of the picture. Her tension had built to a strain. Her eyes were wide open now and staring at the crushed handkerchief. Her petulant mouth no longer pouted. Through the grim mask I thought I saw the shadow of hate.

I said, 'You know the other woman?'

She shook her head. 'That's why I'm hiring you.'

'She'll be on the train?'

Mrs. DePereyra closed her eyes. 'I don't know. I never did know anything about Michael's women friends.'

'He's had others?'

'Yes. He's had many others.'

'Why don't you divorce him?'

Her cold eyes stared at me. 'Your job is just to watch my husband and find out who his girl friend is, do you understand?'

'And after that?'

'After that, you're through.' She opened her purse and pulled out five twenty-dollar bills. She folded them and slid them across the table to me. She was smiling again, the meaningless theatrical smile that meant nothing at all but the prelude to a nervous breakdown or something worse. She put the bills in my palm and held them there. 'Is this enough?'

'It'll hold me,' I said. 'You'll be on the train?'

'I'll be on the train. But you don't know me. Is that clear?'

'That's no lie.'

She got up and adjusted the furs on her shoulders. She made a great show of settling them in just the right position. She leaned over the table to get her purse and gloves and as she bent toward me she smiled again. I watched her walk to the door and when she reached it she turned for a last look at me over her furs, opened the door and went out.

Harry was waiting for me at the bar. 'How does it look, Steve? Anything in it?'

I took one of the twenties out of the small roll and handed it to him. 'A very interesting customer, Harry. The case looks like a pushover.'

'Who pushes who?'

'That's what makes it interesting,' I said. 'You never can tell with a dame like that.'

2

I took another gulp of my highball and stared out of the window. The train was moving fast now. It was black outside and only once in a while a farm window blinked and slid past us in the void. The song of the wheels almost closed my eyes. Almost, but not quite.

The big redhead in the next chair nudged me.

'Look,' she murmured. 'It's that man again.'

I followed her finger. Max Popper stood at the far end of the car. He spotted us, pursed his lips and started toward us.

The redhead said, 'Here comes your quiet friend with the lemons in his mouth. What is he, your father or something, the way he follows you around?'

I said, 'Max? Max is all right. He and I work together.'

She measured him with a slow smile. 'A

10

man like Max should be digging graves or maybe haunting small houses. Or are you in business with the rest of these zombies?'

She was waving an orange-tipped hand at the group of assorted characters around and about us, a motley gathering of all types and ages, a quiet collection of professorial talent. They were bald-pated or gray-topped, heavily eye-glassed, mustached, lined and furrowed in the face and brow. The train was full of them.

I said, 'These gents are a little out of my class, honey. You are looking at a brain convention. These are all members of the atomic energy tribe.'

The redhead bent her frame to survey the car full of talent. She said, 'You'd never know it. They look like a bunch of plumbers.'

'That sums it all up,' I said.

Max turned his back on the girl when he arrived and stood over me with his hands rammed deep into his pants. He looked down at me and pursed his lips and shook his head slowly.

'You figuring on killing the evening this

way, Steve? You want to make a play for this surrey with the fringe on her hips?'

'I'm toying with the idea,' I said. 'But you're not in the way. You could hang around and keep your eye open for DePereyra.'

'You really going to work for that dizzy broad?'

I said, 'She paid. We work.'

Max surveyed the club car with a sleepy eye. 'You work. Me, I'm going back to the room. Even a half-crocked gorilla like you can catch her husband if he walks in. I'm going to get myself some sleep. See you in the morning.'

The redhead watched him go, smiling at his back over her glass. She put the glass down and wiped her mouth with a little lace handkerchief. She worked at the corners of her mouth and then tucked the handkerchief away into the natural pocket in the V of her dress. She said, 'Max is quite a character. What does he do for the great detective, fill your fountain pen for you?'

I said, 'Whatever Max does, he does well. He's got a memory like a sheet of flypaper. He remembers everything: faces, facts, figures and folderol. Max stores it all up. One look at you and he's tucked your face away in a special spot behind his ears. Forty years from now, if you should walk into my office, Max will tell me who you are.'

'Forty years from now you won't want me in your office.'

I squeezed her arm. 'Forty years from now I won't want any dame in my office. Here comes the boy. You want another drink?'

She finished her drink in a gulp and passed her glass. I ordered two more. I leaned back in my seat and closed my eyes and thought about Sybil, who was part of my present and sat near enough to be part of my immediate future. I thought about the blonde who had boarded the train in Chicago, too. It would be pleasanter to be sitting next to the blonde. The blonde was of a different breed.

When the drinks came I opened my eyes and looked at the redhead. Sybil Drake was a tall girl, big-boned but not at all angular. She was pretty in a theatrical sort of way, the type of prettiness that comes off with a rag full of cold cream. She was well rouged around the cheek bones and too blackly mascaraed over the eyes. She was firm and fleshy in the torso and had a small, round head that tilted provocatively when she talked. She had full lips that always seemed moist and never frowned.

Beyond Sybil, I saw the blonde enter the car, alone. She moved gracefully to a chair and sat down. She opened a magazine and pretended to be reading it. I watched her eyes and saw that she wasn't reading it at all. She just sat there staring at the magazine. I leaned back in my chair and pretended to talk to the redhead while I watched the blonde.

I looked at Sybil and talked to Sybil, but my heart wasn't in it any more. Sybil winked at me and smiled. It was a solid smile, loaded with a lot of meaning. I would have given a small slice of my right arm for the same kind of smile from the blonde. But the blonde still studied the magazine. She hadn't turned the page.

Sybil leaned toward me over the arm of her chair, showing me her even teeth and holding her voice low and sweet enough to curl my hair. She purred at me in soft, Bacardi syllables.

Any night but this, the big redhead would have held my eye and ear. Tonight, with the blonde in the car, Sybil was nothing more than a voice and the strong smell of liquor and perfume. I stared again at the little blonde.

But the little blonde didn't stare at me. Now she was engaged in a serious conversation with a tall, Harvard type who leaned forward on a well-creased knee and spoke earnestly with his index finger as well as his mouth. I sat up. It was Michael DePereyra.

There was no laughter between these two. They were discussing something too serious and heavy for a smile or a laugh.

Sybil Drake tapped my right knee, lightly.

'Get me another drink, Detective,' she said. 'Come out of your trance and get me another drink.'

I said, 'I was admiring that silver clip

on your shoulder.'

Sybil fingered the brooch. 'You like it?'

'Prettiest little piece I've seen in a long time. Is it Jensen?'

Sybil laughed in her throat. When she put her hand on my wrist it was cold and damp from the glass it had held. 'It sure is a pretty little piece, big boy. But how did you figure her name is Jensen? You trying to outfox her boy friend? He's a pretty nice-looking hunk of vest and pants, isn't he? That type of gent doesn't move his tail away from a blonde until some muscle man bounces him on his nose. And the little blonde is definitely class, Detective. You don't get a blonde like that by sitting on your can and staring her to death. I can figure her from where I'm sitting. Any woman knows any strange blonde better than any man. That's because a man stops at her face, or her legs, or some other spot that doesn't mean anything. Don't look now, but can you tell me what kind of a dress she's wearing?'

I said, 'It's blue, with silver buttons.'

She laughed at me. 'Now I'm sure you

stopped at her face. The dame is sporting a grayish-blue suit, a little number that set somebody back plenty of rocks, because it comes from DePinna and DePinna wasn't handing those suits out as door prizes the last time I was there. The little piece of fur around her neck is a slice of sable, specially clipped for her lily white neck. The dame is real class. Her hair is natural blonde. I can see it from here because I know that peroxide never made a head shine the way hers does. The silver earrings aren't five and dime items, they come from Mr. Tichaud's place — a small store on Madison Avenue where they won't open the door for you unless they've checked your roll and know your grandfather. She's wearing shoes that came from somewhere in the made-to-order belt and that diamond ring on her left hand is just neat enough to cost plenty. The way her face is made up shows that she's cocky. Any doll with her looks doesn't have to worry about competition. She knows that she can hold her own without polishing her pan with rouge and mascara. From the way she's talking to handsome over there I can tell that she isn't giving him any time. She's just about answering.'

I said, 'You've got a mind like a crystal ball. What was he asking her?'

'If he was asking what you think, she'd probably give him the brush. She's got sharp eyes. She's fruit only when she likes a man.'

'And she doesn't like the man?'

Sybil shook her head. 'She's been playing him, but not for keeps. She's got the kind of face that has a brain behind it. She's clever as hell.'

'You don't like her?'

'A redhead can't afford to like a blonde, Detective. And that one's got plenty on the ball. I wouldn't trust her any further than you could throw her. Oh — oh — look who's coming in!'

3

I watched the Harvard face stand up when a short, dark and pretty woman entered the car and joined him near the blonde. It was my client, Dolly DePereyra. The tableau was obvious: handsome gent discovered talking to handsome blonde by ever-loving woman. The man tried for composure, failed, and went through the pantomime of introducing the newcomer. It was an embarrassed introduction. DePereyra colored while going through it and I caught the suppressed anger in his eyes.

Sybil said, 'If I wanted to do you a favor I could give you a knock down to the doll who just walked in.'

'And you don't want to do me a favor?'

'What'll it get me?'

I squeezed her arm. 'My undying affection, sugar. You know the dame?'

'It could be.'

'Who is she?'

19

'Dolly French,' Sybil said. 'She danced next to me for three years down at The Brass Tack. She was the hottest thing in the world on bumps and grinds and look at her now.'

I said, 'She still looks hot.'

'Dolly's come up in the world. She's fancied up. If I didn't know her so well I'd never have recognized Dolly in that get up. She's heavy with sugar — probably won't even give me the right time.'

I got up and leaned over Sybil. 'How about a try?'

She sighed and eyed me archly. 'What a salesman,' she said.

She shrugged and got up and I followed her. A few professorial heads followed her, too, probably assessing her hips for atomic energy.

Dolly French blinked twice and then threw her arms around her old friend Sybil.

She said, 'Sybil! It's been a long time, hasn't it? This is my husband, Michael DePereyra.'

Michael DePereyra didn't enjoy meeting Sybil, and relished me less. Dolly had never seen me before. There was a confused and awkward round of introductions. The little blonde sat out the byplay. She was finally included in the fiesta of formality and reached up to shake my hand and give me her smile. Her smile and her hand were warm and solid and impersonal. She was Mary Wyndham.

Dolly and Sybil moved off together.

I leaned over Mary Wyndham and DePereyra didn't enjoy the vista of my back. He fiddled with his tie, coughed politely once or twice, bowed and left.

I said, 'Funny about people on trains. You sit in a corner and play games with them. You get tired of reading soupy magazine fiction and put it down and study your fellow passengers. There isn't a parlor game in the world with more laughs. Ever play it?'

She looked down at the magazine in her lap and smiled. 'I suppose I do, once in a while. It isn't an easy game for a woman to play. Some people are liable to misunderstand. Then it becomes an embarrassing pastime.'

She had a soft voice, low and sweet and made to order for easy conversation.

I said, 'A Mary Wyndham could be related to the famous Professor Wyndham — the atomic Wyndham.'

'I'm his niece,' she said. 'That's Uncle Oscar, over there.'

I followed her finger. She was pointing at a man halfway down the car, a dark and handsome man who looked old enough to be her husband.

I said, 'Did you say 'Uncle'?'

'Uncle Oscar is what I said.'

I whistled. 'How does he do it? Or is he as young as I think he is?'

'The Wyndhams are famous for the size of their family and the good looks of their men.'

'And women,' I added. 'How do they do it?'

'He's the youngest uncle I have — and the nicest and the cleverest. He's kept his youth by working hard, he says. He's still going strong, and getting more famous by the minute.'

'He's part of the shindig going into New York for the conference?'

She nodded. 'You'll be reading a lot about him from now on.'

'The big boy you were talking to. Is he part of the shindig, too?'

She shrugged it away.

I said, 'Funny, about him. I never would have pegged him as a Michael DePereyra. He didn't hit me that way at all.'

She laughed again. When she laughed her eyes closed tight and made pretty little wrinkles that added to her girlishness.

'How did you peg him?'

'I figured him for an overgrown college boy.'

'You talk like a detective.'

'Maybe I am a detective.'

'If you are, you're a bad one,' she smiled. 'You've made your deductions on the basis of remote observation. You've given him a character reading from forty-paces and out of the dialogue of a simple introduction.'

'When I say college boy I don't really mean college boy. Sometimes I don't even mean college. A man can break his neck trying to make people believe he's a type of perennial college boy, do you follow me?'

She followed me. She followed me so well that I found myself running to keep alongside her. She said, 'You're prejudiced. A good detective shouldn't be prejudiced. You don't like college boys?'

'I never said I didn't like him.'

'You don't have to say it. You've been sitting over there gawking at him over your liquor glass.'

'I plead not guilty. I was staring at you.'

'At me?' she said, just as though she didn't believe it. 'Now why would a detective be staring at me?'

She was easier than I thought she would be. I sat down and leaned toward her. 'I can give you a few dozen reasons. Do you want them all now or should I spread them out over a period of months?'

'Why should you spread them out?'

'I'd enjoy it,' I said.

'What's the next move?'

'Dinner?'

'I'm sorry,' she said, as though she

24

meant it. 'I've already had my dinner and now I've got to do a bit of paper work for Professor Wyndham. Try me again in a few hours. I might allow myself a nightcap.'

'I'll be here,' I said.

'Of course you will.'

I went into the diner and found Sybil waiting for me. She had the look of a cat who has swallowed a canary, cage and all. She said, 'You got here sooner than I figured. She must have given you a very quick brush.'

The car filled up with assorted atomic talent while we ate. The hum of their double-talk filled my ears.

Sybil toyed with her dessert. 'Where do you hang out in New York?'

'I have a small office under my hat.'

Sybil wiped her lips daintily. She lit a cigarette and struck an advertising billboard pose. She watched the smoke for a while and then killed the butt, suddenly. She looked at her wristwatch, sighed and stood up.

'It's getting late, Detective. We pull into Grand Central early and I've got a heavy day tomorrow. Look me up some rainy Thursday night.'

I watched her hips until they were lost beyond the line of heads in the diner. She turned at the end of the car, stood there for a moment and telegraphed a slow smile and a slower wink to me. It would have been nice to get up and follow her. My legs were all for it, but my brain held them under the table and I just sat there struggling with my better man.

I ordered a drink and sat fondling it until it disappeared. I ordered a small pot of coffee and spent another half hour finishing it and contemplating the black nothingness of the landscape.

I lent half an ear to the hum of conversation around me. The buzz began to annoy me and I moved back into the club car. The few magazines scattered around the place didn't keep me awake long. My consciousness soon gave up the idea of waiting, like a keyed-up college boy, for the theoretical entrance of Mary Wyndham.

The last time I looked at my watch it was after ten o'clock and a few strays were entering the car for a short conversational bout before bedtime. I closed my eyes and let the drone of their voices lull me to sleep.

I woke suddenly. Somebody was patting my face.

The patting was not slapping, but it was deliberate and insistent.

The hands belonged to Sybil Drake.

She was dressed in an elegant yellow robe, cut to display the niceties of her midsection.

I said, 'I'm sorry I kept you waiting, honey. I'll be with you as soon as I rub the sand out of my eyes.'

She patted my face a little harder, almost slap heavy. She kept slapping it until I sat up straight and grabbed her hands. She wasn't smiling. Her face was pale and unpainted. Her eyes had lost their mascara depths and were wide open with fright.

Her voice matched her eyes. 'Wake up, Detective! It's Dolly DePereyra! She's going nuts!'

I said, 'Give it to me again, slow and easy.'

'Dolly's in my room, Steve, screaming something about her husband. I thought maybe you could quiet her down and find out where the pin is sticking. She scared the pants off me. She scared me so bad I ran out of the room. I can't stand a hysterical woman.'

She ran through the empty club car with much more speed than I thought she could muster. We raced through two more cars and Sybil stopped at a door.

'I'll wait here,' she said. 'When I look at her my stomach does funny things and I feel faint.'

I found Dolly on Sybil's berth, face down, sobbing her heart out into the pillow. Her fists were clenched and she punctuated her stifled screams by systematically banging the flesh off her knuckles on the wall.

I grabbed her hands and managed to turn her a bit. She squirmed away from me and dove for the pillow. I reached under her heaving torso and gently pulled her around. When she tried to get away from me I used force. She chewed her lip and moaned into the shreds of what was once a lace handkerchief. She bent forward and held her head and sobbed.

I knelt beside her and tried to break through the barrier of sheer hysteria. The sobbing was low pitched and hoarse now. She didn't open her eyes at all.

Sybil came in and said: 'She's been that way for almost a half hour.'

'That's not good.'

I slapped her across the face once, not hard, but not too gently.

'Michael!' she wailed. 'Oh, Michael, Michael, Michael!'

'What about Michael?'

She burbled a few unintelligible sentences, heavy with sobs and emotional syllables. She gasped this double-talk until my knees hurt.

Sybil plucked at my sleeve, motioned me out of the room.

'That type of dame won't calm down until she's good and ready. You're wasting your time.'

I said: 'Where's her room?'

We ran along the corridor. The first gray fingers of dawn were pointing up the hills and bathing the landscape in a dirty light. We paused two cars down and Sybil put her hand to her throat. There was a compartment door ahead, half ajar.

'Wait here,' I told her. 'I'll be right out.'

I ran past her into the compartment and almost tripped over the body on the floor.

It was Michael DePereyra. He was smeared in an incongruous pose, head staring at the ceiling. I leaned over him and put my ear to his vest. There was no beat. My ear hit a hard object in his vest pocket. It was a small package of film; a small yellow box. I lifted it out of his pocket and tucked it away. I knelt there for a moment, wondering whether I should return it. In the split second of decision, I decided against putting it back.

Sybil was waiting for me tremblingly.

'You're as green as a dollar bill,' she said. 'What's up?'

'Plenty, sugar, plenty. I found our chum Michael loused up on the floor in there.'

'Drunk?'

'Stiff. Dead. No wonder your friend Dolly is chewing the edges off her lip. She's in trouble — plenty of trouble.'

4

I tapped Max Popper on the shoulder and he sat up. When Max awoke there were never any preliminaries. His brain opened for business just as soon as his eyes did. There were no yawns, no stretches, no eye-rubs; no fogbound sentences.

Max said, 'It's not even light yet and you're standing there all dressed up. Where the hell have you been all night, on your ear in that club chair?'

I watched him lace his shoes and marveled at his early morning dexterity. I said, 'I just tripped over a dead man.'

Max looked up for only a second. 'You're always tripping over things. Who killed him?'

'I don't know. Maybe he wasn't killed. Maybe he died of heart trouble.'

'So he died of heart trouble. Is that why you come in here waking me up at this hour? Or did you get in a jam on account of that big broad you were ear-bending last night?'

'Sybil is all right,' I said, and explained what had happened.

Max said, 'You figure DePereyra's wife killed him?'

'I'm not interested. I figured I'd get you up so that you could nose around. There may be something in this thing for us, I don't know. We'll pull into New York in a little while and we'll hit Mrs. Brunick for her payoff on the L. A. job and from there on out we've got nothing worth much except that old lady in Brooklyn with the missing uncle. Or don't you follow me?'

Max slid into his jacket and straightened his tie. He parted his thinning hair before the mirror, put the comb away, adjusted the handkerchief in his breast pocket and then just stood there staring at me.

I handed him the package of film and told him to hold it. Max scowled at it and stuffed it away in a pocket. 'French pictures?' he asked.

'Maybe. We won't know until we print

them. They may be worth some dough to us.'

'What do you want me to do now?' Max said.

'Sybil broke down after I told her about DePereyra,' I said. 'I had to take her to the club car — she wouldn't go back to Dolly because she couldn't stand her routine.'

Max sucked an imaginary lemon. 'You're not telling me to keep the big babe company, are you?'

'You're too wide-awake, Max. I've got a tougher job for you. Go down to Sybil's room and start unbuttoning Mrs. DePereyra's brain. Tell her as much as you have to tell her. See if you can draw her out a little. You may be able to get something we can use sometime.'

Max hesitated in the corridor. He stared out of the window. 'You sure you know what you're doing, Steve? It doesn't smell too pretty for a couple of hungry eyes to be lousing around with stuff like this.'

'Let me do the worrying.'

'Sure. Sure, I'll let you worry. Like the

last time. We're pulling into New York, remember. New York is a big town and they have big cops and big cops are tough cops. We don't want to get jerked around like what happened to us a couple months ago. The side of my head still hurts from that last session.'

'Stay there until I arrive. Everybody on the train is asleep. Nobody will bother you.'

'I get it — nobody bothers Maxie. And you? Where will you be?'

'I'm on my way to find a doctor.'

Two cars away a drowsy porter informed me that he had a doctor in a lower berth. I watched him rouse the sleeping medico and stood back until a little man in a purple robe stepped out into the aisle.

He was gray-eyed, as high as my elbow and up to his ears in dream dust. His name was Doctor Emanuel and he was anxious to please. He followed me through the train as though I had him on a leash.

I motioned him inside DePereyra's room and he stepped around the corpse gingerly, uttering low bird calls. He prodded the body. He got down on his knees and whistled once or twice.

When he stood up he was shaking his head and clucking sympathetically.

I said, 'What's the matter with the man?'

'Everything. Friend of yours?'

'I never saw him before I noticed his door open on my way to my room. What's with him?'

He made up his professional face, eyes wide open and dead pan. 'This man is dead.'

I sucked in some air in a mock try at horror. 'Dead? How terrible! How long has he been dead, Doctor?'

'Not too long, I'd judge.' He took out a little red book and began to scribble a few notes. He paused and eyed me speculatively. 'I'd suggest that you remain here until I get the porter.'

He stood in the corridor. He took off his glasses and polished them on the sash of his robe. He fished into his pocket and came up with the notebook again.

'Your name?' he asked. 'I'd better put

your name down — just for the officials.'

I gave him my name and he moved off down the corridor.

When he had passed out of sight, I stepped back into DePereyra's room nimbly. I kneeled over the corpse and commenced a rapid frisk. My hand avoided the familiar objects, groped for the unusual. He carried nothing appealing in his outer pockets. I pulled out his wallet, a slick pigskin affair of the oversized variety. There were many bills. In one compartment, there was a small wad of note-paper. I pocketed the scraps and replaced his wallet.

I skirted the corpse and began to take inventory. The lower berth was disarranged. Somebody had used it last night, although the disarray was casual and suggested a short stay on the bedding and not beneath it.

The upper berth was untouched, sheets and blankets smooth, pillow unruffled. There was a small leather suitcase on the floor.

I opened the suitcase and ruffled through the odds and ends of feminine apparel. I dug deeper and found the expected layer of cosmetics and decorative folderol all women carry with them on journeys. I dropped my hand among these things.

My hand felt the expected shapes. There were many bottles of cold cream, nail polish and several cardboard containers of powder. There was a lipstick case and a small jewel case. These slid through my fingers quickly, as quickly as my brain could catalogue them.

But my hand tightened, finally, over a familiar shape. I lifted it and stared at it in the gloom. I tucked it away into a pocket. This bottle was different. It was of the ordinary drugstore variety, longish and heavy and just the size for iodine or some other pharmaceutical concoction. Like poison.

My back was to the door so that I could not see who hit me. My last live memory was the sound of a foot-fall and then the stinging pain behind my ear. I floated off into a miasma of bright and shining shapes, some in technicolor. I dropped into this void and stayed there.

I had been sapped. But good.

I awoke slowly, climbing through the buzz in my brain to face the buzz above and about me. Several dozen people danced before my eyes, most of whom were Doctor Emanuel and the colored porter and two other strange gentlemen who stared at me with great interest.

The doctor slapped my face tenderly with a wet rag; the porter just stood there and made no comment.

I waved away the wet rag and managed to sit up. I felt for my head and made it. My fingers touched a large and growing lump behind my ear.

The doctor said, 'You've been hit, but it isn't too bad. Nothing open or bleeding.'

'Fine,' I said. 'That's just dandy.'

'Who hit you?' asked one of the strange gentlemen. He was a tall, thin, serious man. His voice floated down to me, a gentle voice, full of sympathy and curiosity.

'Isn't the victim supposed to ask that question? I don't know who hit me, but if I ever catch up with him I'm going to shake his hand. It was a neat job. How long have I been out?'

The doctor said, 'I've only been gone a few minutes. I should say that whoever hit you must have seen me go.'

'A good guess, doc.' I felt in my pockets. My wallet hadn't been touched. I had just as little money as ever. My few assorted papers were intact. And the little drugstore bottle still reposed in my jacket. Whoever hit me was after bigger game than my wallet or my papers or the little bottle. Whoever hit me was well muscled and in a great hurry.

The porter said, 'Nobody passed us when we were coming into the car. But this gentleman here says he saw somebody.'

The other man stepped forward. He was of medium height. He looked down at me through heavy lenses. Through the lenses his eyes were cow-like and out of proportion to his gnome face.

When he talked, his beetle brows oscillated. 'Professor McCormack and I were on the way back to our room. I walked ahead of him as we entered this car. I am quite sure I saw a man come out of this room and run up the corridor. Quite sure.'

'And who are you?' I asked.

'I am Professor John Frotti,' he said, as though I were a student who didn't know his lesson. 'And this is Professor McCormack.'

'Delighted,' I said. 'And how is it you two were up so early in the morning?'

McCormack smiled at Frotti. Frotti glared at me, glared at McCormack, glared at me again. 'I see no reason for answering your impertinent questions, young man.'

McCormack continued to smile. 'There's no need for temper, John. Nor is there any necessity for withholding information from this gentleman. The reason why we are up so early in the morning is quite obvious. We just didn't go to bed. John and I and another colleague, a man named Gunther, were simply talking. You might call it a business talk. We lost ourselves in our own chatter, became so engrossed in our discussion that we completely forgot about sleep. That happens often, young man, when a good argument gets going.'

'Thank you,' I said. 'Now let's start all over again.' I turned to Frotti. 'You saw somebody on the way out of this compartment?'

Frotti nodded. 'I did.'

'What did he look like?'

'I don't know. I didn't see his face.'

'And you, Professor McCormack?'

McCormack smiled his gentle smile and shook his head. 'I saw nobody. I entered the car a few minutes after Professor Frotti, you see.'

Frotti began to puff. He eyed his colleague with sudden anger. Through his heavy lenses the anger was emphasized, enlarged, exaggerated. 'What do you mean by that, McCormack?'

'Mean?'

'You were behind me, weren't you?'

'Oh, no,' said the other, gently. 'I wasn't that close to you, John. I had stopped in the next car, to say goodnight to Gunther, you remember.'

'I remember nothing!' Frotti shouted. 'I took for granted the fact that you had followed me into this car.'

'Tut, tut, John. Isn't that a peculiarly

unscientific assumption?'

'Ridiculous! You were right behind me!'

McCormack shrugged. 'Gunther will prove you wrong, I'm sure.'

I said, 'Let it pass. You didn't see the man's face, Frotti?'

He shook his head, violently. 'I did not.'

'What did you see?'

'A man. I saw a man.'

'A tall man?'

'I cannot say whether he was tall or short. I did not measure him. He was running away.'

'You didn't see his face, then?'

'I saw only his back.'

'Oh, fine,' I said. 'You're a big help, Frotti. You saw a man, yet you didn't see him. He wasn't tall or short, and for your money he didn't even have a face. He didn't happen to be a friend of yours, did he?'

'I resent that!' shouted Frotti, and adjusted his features to promote his resentment. 'I don't like your insinuations!'

'And I don't like your testimony. That makes us even. You're doing me as much good as another lump on the head. Or am I offending you again?'

McCormack interceded for his friend. 'You must remember that John's eyes are bad.'

'My eyes are very bad,' said Frotti. 'Any fool would deduce that fact by simply examining my lenses.'

I said: 'I'm idiot enough to have taken your glasses into consideration, Frotti. But you're testifying like a blind man. How about the suit he wore. The color?'

'I cannot help you, I'm afraid. It was a dark suit; that is all.'

'Blue? Brown?'

'It was dark.'

I turned to the porter.

'Who's bedded down in this car, Porter?' I asked.

'The car is taken up with the scientific party, sir. That is, for the most part it is. Mr. and Mrs. DePereyra are the exceptions.'

'And there is a fellow named Folsom, too, who isn't a scientist,' said McCormack. 'I know this because I met the gentleman.'

'You met him on the train?'

He nodded. 'Tonight. A nice enough sort of chap — a merchant from New York. Dry goods, I think he said.'

'Where is he?'

'I left him back in the club car.'

Frotti snorted and diddled with his mustache.

I said, 'How many cars up ahead of this one, Porter?'

'Only three.'

I massaged the lump behind my ear, tenderly. 'Three cars too many. Can I stand up now, Doctor?'

'You can try.'

I made it. I leaned against the door and surveyed the compartment through the small fog that played around my eyes. The compartment seemed the same. The corpse still lay in the same place.

The porter said, 'I'll have to inform the chief conductor about this. I don't imagine there is anything he can do about it until we get into New York.'

'When does that happen?'

'In about an hour or so. Is there anything I can do for you until then, sir?'

'What I need now is a stiff medicinal dose of whiskey followed by a cold shower. You know where to reach me, Porter.'

I turned to leave, but didn't quite make it. Max Popper was arriving, walking fast. He was wearing a new face, especially made up to convince everybody that he was a very worried man.

'Where can I find a doctor, gents?' Max asked. 'I need a doctor right away!'

'You, too?' I asked. 'Who slugged you?'

'Nobody slugged me. It's that dame.'

The scene was as pat as a sequence from a bad movie. Doctor Emanuel put his hands behind his back and drew himself up to his full five feet two.

'I am a doctor, my good man,' he said. 'What seems to be the trouble?'

'It's not me, Doc,' said Max, and opened his eyes wide to show his innocent worriment. 'It's a lady in the other car. I just saw her pass out cold!'

5

It was 9:03 by the big clock in Grand Central Station.

Max and I stood at the right side of the gate, away from the exit. The early morning traffic slid past us in a never-ending stream, but we were out of it. Our backs to the marble wall, we surveyed the scene with ease and detachment. My eyes held down a small square of space around the gate to the Chicago train that had just brought us into New York. Every once in a while a group of people came out of that gate.

Max said, 'What are we waiting for?'

'Dolly French,' I said. 'Dolly DePereyra.'

'Don't kid me, Steve. What would you want with that fruitcake?'

'I've got ideas,' I said. 'And she paid us money.'

Max grunted. 'I got ideas, too. I got an

idea you're parking your can here to catch something else.'

A group of two reporters and a cameraman came out of the gate, followed by four men. The four men stood there awkwardly, shifting their weight around uneasily. The cameraman stepped forward and grouped them. He walked backward, slowly, holding up a finger. The four men smiled. The camera snapped.

I said, 'That should be the last of the atom scientists. Dolly will be along any minute.'

'You and your Dolly,' said Max. 'Is it really Dolly, or are you expecting that blonde?'

I turned to thump him playfully on the shoulder. 'Look, Max, that blonde left the train while the fat dick was grilling me. I saw her walk down the corridor with her little suitcase on the way out. And, before you ask me, I'm not waiting for Sybil Drake, either. She stayed behind with her friend Dolly. She went soft and decided to take care of her. Any more ideas?'

Max shrugged, fussed with a package of cigarettes.

I couldn't blame him for being upset. It was the fat dick who had upset him. Other things had upset Max, too.

The fat dick was Jim Heath, a New York homicide man who had a habit of spitting at you when he asked you questions. Heath had held us for too long. He had beaten down our self-respect with a stupid routine.

Heath had enjoyed playing with Max. He was very curious about Max's visit to Sybil's room. He teased Max. He suggested that Max explain why Mrs. DePereyra fainted. He tried to build up the theory that Max was on the make for Dolly. There were hard, hot words between Max and Heath.

It all ended, finally, and we were allowed to go home. It was then that we ran into the press.

A covey of news quail had come down to the station to interview the atomic bigwigs. There were many familiar faces in the mob, among them Lester Henshaw, an old saloon friend. Lester ate up the story of Michael DePereyra. Lester figured it would rate space because of the atomic bunch. I didn't understand Lester. That, however, didn't matter to Lester. He cornered me on the platform and held me there until he had enough facts for an angle story. He went even further. He had his photographer tail us up the ramp and snap our picture as we passed through the gate. When the flashlight bulb went off, Max uttered an obscenity and chased the lens man all the way out of the station. He returned breathless and on fire with unbridled disgust.

I didn't blame him. I said, 'I don't blame you for being mad, Max. But I may have something with Dolly DePereyra.'

'A pitch?'

'A big pitch,' I said. 'She didn't spill to you because she was hysterical.'

'If she wasn't, she made a damned good attempt at proving herself batty. That fruitcake is either Greta Garbo or just plain nuts. I don't like playing games with dames like that. I have more fun in an empty closet, talking to myself.' Max finally lit his cigarette and glared at me through the first smoke cloud. 'What kind of a pitch?'

'A little bottle from a drugstore. In her valise.'

'You got it?'

I patted my coat. Max laughed out loud. I laughed, too.

Max stopped laughing. 'Quit playing tag with me, Steve. What's in the bottle, cough medicine?'

'Maybe. Little bottles don't usually hold enough medicine, though. I like to think of little drugstore bottles holding arsenic, or strychnine, or other appetizers of that variety. I keep asking myself foolish questions about this deal. Why was the bottle of poison left in my pocket? If the gent who slugged me wasn't after the poison, what did he bat me around for? Was he after that roll of film? And if he wanted that film, we're off on another tangent that doesn't make sense at all.'

I was facing the gate as we talked. I watched the gate casually, as though I didn't have a reason for watching. The small knot of people who had been waiting for friends on the train had long since met their friends and disappeared into the nether reaches of the station. Yet, there were still a few people hanging around. There was a young boy in a Navy uniform, reading a paper and glancing up at the clock every once in a while. There were a man and a woman, off to one side, talking earnestly near the gate.

And there was the woman in the leopard coat.

I watched the woman in the leopard coat. She was a youngish woman, medium-sized. She had fine, rounded hips. The leopard coat was cut to promote those hips. The leopard coat was half open, as if she had intended to use it as a fashion model would use it — open in front to display the dress beneath. The dress was well worth featuring. It was a simple number, so simple that it held my eyes at her chest and made it tough for me to assess her face.

Her face was of the black and white variety. She wore a lot of powder, but little rouge, and the effect was startling because her features were so beautiful. She had dark eyes. She played games with her eyes. She pretended that she wasn't interested in the Chicago gate. She stole a glance at the gate at regular intervals and then focused on our wall, the far wall and, finally, the clock. It was fun watching her.

Max said, 'Look! Your girl friend Sybil is coming out with Dolly!'

I looked, but not at Sybil and Dolly. The woman in the leopard coat began to fascinate me, suddenly. When she saw Dolly, she turned on her heel and made a great show of dropping her purse. She bent over for the purse and seemed in no hurry to recover it. When Dolly and Sybil passed, she stepped backward a few paces and bit her lower lip.

I said, 'Wait here, Max. I've got a job to do.'

I walked over to the gate and peered down the ramp. I shook my head sadly and stepped to within five feet of the leopard coat. I waited for her eye, got it and moved in.

I said, 'You're not Midge Tucker, are you?'

She was not Midge Tucker. She shook

52

her head and didn't smile.

I said, 'I hope you'll forgive me.'

'I'll forgive you,' she said. 'Now go away.'

'This Midge Tucker,' I went on, 'I've never met her. She came in on that Chicago train and my boss sent me here to pick her up — '

'Did your boss tell you to pick up a substitute?' she asked, giving me a close-up of her back and her beautiful hips. 'You'd better start moving, big boy.'

'I'm sorry,' I said, as though I was sorry. 'I'm not on the make, young lady. I guess I got here a bit too late to catch Miss Tucker. I suppose that business on the train upset her, anyway, the poor kid. All that excitement on the train — '

She grabbed the hook. She turned my way, slowly, and gave me her big black eyes.

'Excitement?' she asked. 'What excitement?'

Her guard was down now. She took a tentative step toward me.

I said, 'Didn't you hear about all the fuss on that train? Gosh, they had a flock of reporters all over the place.'

'The reporters were down here to get those professors,' she snapped. 'What other excitement was there?'

'I know,' I said, and played my dialogue soft and stupid. 'But then there was that man who died, and all.'

She put a hand on my arm, suddenly. 'What man?'

'The man who died?' I went through a three-round wrestling match with my memory. I watched her as I stalled. She was on edge now. I held her there for a moment. 'He had a funny name. Sort of a foreign name, they told me. Can't quite recall it.'

'A foreign name? Like what? Was it Spanish?'

I studied the floor, trying to find the name in the marble. I gave up the floor and concentrated on the ceiling mural. Her hand was tighter on my arm now.

'Think!' she begged me. 'Was it a Spanish name?'

'That's it, exactly. His name was something like DePinada, or DePeralda, or — '

'DePereyra?'

'That's it! Gosh, don't tell me you knew the poor fellow?'

She stood there for a long moment, fighting for composure. She didn't quite make it. She began to tremble a little and her hand left my arm and twitched a bit. She turned away from me, finally, and ran off toward the Vanderbilt Avenue exit.

I motioned to Max and he came running over.

I said, 'Tail that dame in the leopard coat. Keep after her all day. Get me the works on her, but don't let her know it.'

Max didn't pause to react. I watched him climb the steps to the exit. He caught her easily. He was leaving a scientific gap between them so that he could operate.

I walked back to the wall and picked up my bag and headed across the station for a cup of coffee.

6

I stood in the phone booth for fifteen minutes, fiddling with the dial. I rang Mrs. DePereyra's number twelve times in all, allowing a reasonable interval for each signal. I smoked cigarettes and kept ringing Mrs. DePereyra's apartment and listening to the flat buzz at the other end. Nobody answered the phone at Mrs. DePereyra's menage.

I walked around the station for twenty minutes, making a wide, slow tour of the place, enjoying the tide of human traffic, and returning finally to the same phone booth. I called her number twice again. I stood in the booth and meditated until the smoke from my cigarette forced me out.

I checked my bag at the station and walked out into 42nd Street.

Along 42nd Street I held a slow pace, idling at store windows, breathing deep of the crisp fall air and tossing around a few ideas. When I reached Times Square I had made up my mind.

I took a cab to Harry Bender's store. Harry greeted me personally and led me behind the drug counter to his inner sanctum, his pharmaceutical catacomb. It was a familiar den. Harry and I had idled away many a Saturday afternoon playing two-handed pinochle among the drugs and packaged goods.

I handed him the small bottle. I said: 'You're a druggist, chum. Here's a little bottle for you to play with.'

'You want me to swallow it?'

'I want you to tell me what it is.'

Harry uncorked the bottle and sniffed it, tentatively. He closed his eyes and smiled. He held it to the light, poured some of it into a small saucer and performed a quick professional breakdown.

After a while, he said: 'It's arsenic, Steve. It's murder.'

I said: 'I'm an idiot about poisons, Harry. I'm as unprofessional about poison as you are about pinochle. Tell me more. A gent takes some of this vicious vodka. What next?'

'Nothing but trouble. Violent pain, almost immediately. Very horrible. Some victims vomit, others just pass out moaning and reaching for the infinite.'

'How is it doled out?'

Harry laughed. He took off his glasses so that he could enjoy his laughter. 'How? You don't throw arsenic at people. You dose them, Steve, you dose them. It's a convenient poison. It'll go well in any drink, in any food.'

'Liquor?'

'It works admirably in liquor.'

'They can't taste it?'

'Not when it's brewed this way. This stuff is absolutely tasteless and twice as colorless.'

I showed him the small roll of film and he promised to have it developed for me quickly. I thanked him and folded a bill into his hand.

It was one o'clock when I left Harry's store and began my aimless stroll through the busy streets of the big town. At two o'clock, I found myself in a small restaurant, at a small table, munching a small sandwich and pondering the small wad of notes I had taken from Michael DePereyra's wallet.

Unfolded, the sheets were tiny pages from a loose-leaf notebook. The perforations were regular, the paper was ruled, and the information on the pages was written in an over-slanted hand:

'G. to make final contact with B. soon.'
'See G. after N. Y.'
'Money from G.? ? ? ?'

There was a telegram, signed by the same 'G.' The yellow sheet was fresh, though folded to match the size of the note paper. The telegram had been received recently. The address on the yellow sheet had been ripped away, but the message was intact:

HAVE YOU GOT FILM STOP TIME SHORT STOP BUTLER KNOWN STOP ISLAND SHOULD BE READY STOP HURRY

G.

I pondered the loose code and got nowhere with it. Who was Butler? And why should the island be ready? And what did all this mean to Mr. G.? There were too many things I didn't know. I decided to begin my education.

On the way to Sybil's I played with the set-up, worrying it for angles. I gave up after a while. The whole affair was too confusing, too well screened. It was the missing foundation of basic cranial footwork that annoyed me.

Sybil lived in the midtown area, in one of the newer and more modernistic cliff dwellings on the west side of the park, in the upper Seventies.

A doorman disguised as Admiral Halsey opened the cab door for me, accepted a dollar bill from me, pushed the lobby door for me, pointed out the elevator to me and would have kissed me good-bye if I hadn't asked him whether Mrs. Sybil Drake had arrived at home. He gave me his dollar smile and informed me that Mrs. Drake had arrived, indeed, only an hour or so ago and I could find her in apartment 816.

Sybil met me at the door to her apartment. She was already in her bedroom clothes, a gossamer outfit as opaque as a sheet of cellophane. Her face lacked make-up and her eyes were tired and worried. She greeted me with a mixture of surprise and vexation.

'So soon, Detective?' she asked herself. 'I didn't figure you for the early afternoon type. I must have been too, too charming last night.'

I walked in smiling. 'You don't know your own strength, honey.'

She took my topcoat and fondled my hat. She stood there for a minute, trying my motive on for size, measuring my dirty mind and all the time smiling at me with what she thought was an imitation of Mona Lisa.

She said, 'Make yourself at home while I put your duds away. I'll get you a drink and we can talk the whole thing over.'

She disappeared through a door on the right and I strolled into her living room. It was a fantasy in red and white, a striped pepperminty decor, probably dreamed up by some sugar-boy decorator. I placed myself in a chair that looked like a barber's awning and took a cigarette from a blood-red box on a modern end table. At the far end of the room, a red-and-white-striped screen partially hid the window. It partially hid a small valise, too.

Sybil faced me on the red couch. There was room for me on the red-and-white-striped cushions, so I joined her there.

She made a small face. 'Don't you ever sleep? After last night I figured you were home in bed. But, no, here you are, as large as life and twice as anxious.'

I said, 'You don't look sleepy, either — you look dead. What's bothering you?'

'Only you, Detective.'

I leaned toward her, but she didn't welcome me. I said, 'It's your passionate furniture that's murdering me, honey. I really only came up for a friendly visit.'

'Close your eyes and talk, then,' she said.

'Not yet, honey. There's something missing.'

'Can the double-talk, big boy. On you it sounds phony. What are you driving at?'

'Dolly,' I said. 'Get Dolly.'

'Oh my God!' Sybil got up and put her

hands on her hips and began to laugh. 'You really are a detective, aren't you?'

'I told you I was. Where's Dolly? Sleeping it off?'

She came over to me and folded her hands across her big bosom and stared at me long and hard. I smiled up at her sweetly.

She said, 'For Christ's sake, why don't you leave the kid alone? All right, you're smart. You're a big, strong, smart eye and you guessed Dolly on the nose. The kid nearly fainted after that lousy cop got through with her. I practically had to carry her out of the station, she was so weak. She didn't want to go home to an empty place with her pretty-puss husband dead in the morgue. So I brought her up here and gave her a little drink and put her to bed. She's in there now. She just fell asleep a couple of minutes ago. And now you come barging in here making with the sex appeal and getting ready to play detective again.'

I let her finish. Then I said, 'You'd better get Dolly out here, sugar. This is serious.'

'So it's serious. Can't you wait a few hours?'

'It's bigger than you think.'

She sat down next to me, so close that I could smell the musk. She leaned on her hands and looked me in the eye again. 'What is it with Dolly?'

'Get her out here. I won't hurt her.'

'You're beginning to make me feel like a damned fool for ever bringing her up here.' She stood up and shrugged. 'Maybe you're right, though. Maybe I'd better get her out of bed.'

When she started for the door, I said, 'No tricks, honey. I know where she lives. I can track her down easily. Maybe what I've got to say to her is nothing at all. Don't tell her I'm here. Just wake her and walk her in to me.'

Sybil opened a red door and walked out of the room. I closed my eyes. The red was beginning to bother my inner man. I remembered reading an article about the effect of color schemes on the libido. Green was soothing, and blue was restful, and red — ? Red was Sybil. I heard her stirring in the room beyond. Dolly's voice, high and querulous, added confusion to the muffled dialogue.

Dolly DePereyra entered, looking like a caricature of herself. She was wearing pajamas, neatly tailored to her trim figure.

She looked a dozen years older than she had last night. Her little eyes were sacked and she would have sprained all the muscles of her face if she had smiled.

Sybil flitted across the room like a mother bird. She hastily filled a glass with scotch and soda and put it in Dolly's hand. Dolly managed a few steps to the chair I had abandoned and sat down on the edge of it.

Sybil said, 'The kid is worn out. She's been through hell.'

I said, 'I can see that. I didn't come here to bother her. I think I can help her.'

Dolly lifted the glass and made it to her mouth. She said, 'I'm afraid I must have made a fool of myself in Sybil's room last night.'

'In Sybil's room?'

'I mean when I carried on about Michael.'

'I understand,' I said, because I didn't

understand, 'But tell me more.'

She put down the glass and brought the handkerchief to her nose. It was a reflex gesture. She didn't cry.

'More? What do you mean?'

I got up and went over to her. I said, 'Look, Dolly French — I'm not going to bite your head off. I'm going to ask you a few questions. All I want is information.'

'Information?' Her voice was more composed now and she raised her chin without too much strain. 'About Michael?'

I nodded. I returned to the couch and sat down and said: 'Your husband was a young man, Dolly. He looked pretty healthy to me. He was healthy, wasn't he?'

Dolly squirmed a bit. Sybil went over to her and sat on the arm of her chair. She put her arm around Dolly's shoulder. She said: 'You might as well talk, honey.'

Dolly stared at the far edge of the carpet. She spent considerable time going over the design. She raised her head, finally. 'Michael was perfectly healthy. We were married for five years and he never went to a doctor in all that time.'

'Fine,' I said. 'No heart trouble? He was too young for heart trouble?'

'He was twenty-seven years old,' she said. 'You're kidding about the heart trouble, aren't you?'

'I'm not kidding. I want to know.'

She shook her head. 'The answer is no. Michael was as strong as a bull.'

'That simplifies things,' I said and began to pace. I chewed a knuckle until I reached the far end of the room, near the screen. I stood there, put my hands behind my back and registered heavy thought. The silence told me that they were watching me closely. I turned and walked slowly back to face Dolly. She was stiffly attentive now.

I said, 'I think Michael was murdered.'

Either her surprise was genuine or she had learned much more than hip shaking in her theatrical career.

'Murdered?' she whispered to herself. 'That can't be true. That can't be true.'

'Why not? He had no enemies?'

She shook her head slowly. 'No enemies. Not Michael.'

67

'How can you be sure? Every man has enemies.'

'Not Michael. I'm sure.'

'He had many friends?'

She shook her head again. She was using a small, well-oiled hinge at the base of her brain. She just sat there shaking her head and looking as white and cold and empty as a new icebox.

She continued to whisper. 'Michael had very few friends.'

'You're talking of men friends?'

She nodded, very quickly and very nervously. 'Of course.'

'And the women? How about Michael's women friends?'

It was like touching the starting button of an electric motor. Dolly began to tremble again, violently. She buried her head in her hands and sobbed. She sat there making funny noises in her throat. Sybil patted her lightly on the back and glared at me.

I said, 'You told me he had women friends. No need to break yourself up over it, Dolly.'

Sybil answered for her. 'Dolly told me

last night that Michael was on the make for a blonde. Your blonde girl friend!'

'Interesting. Did he know her?'

'Did he have to know her?'

'A silly question, sugar,' I smiled at Sybil. 'It might mean something if he knew Mary Wyndham.'

'Nuts!' said Sybil. 'He probably knew her the way you did. He was just on the make for her!'

'An idea, but how can we be sure he didn't actually know her better than I did?'

Dolly was loosening up, following every line of our dialogue. 'Maybe you're right — maybe Michael did know her. She might have murdered him!'

'Not Mary Wyndham,' I said.

'Phoo!' said Sybil. 'Now he's an expert on Mary Wyndham! What do you know about this Wyndham wren, Detective?'

'I know what I like,' I laughed. 'You're just jealous, sugar.'

'Me, jealous?' Sybil twittered. 'I'm never jealous of that kind of blonde, Junior. Suspicious, yes.'

'You're whistling in the dark.'

'I never whistled at a blonde in my life!'

I said, 'You don't know, do you, Dolly? You can't be sure that he never met this blonde before she got on the train?'

'I never knew anything about Michael, really. Sure — I suspected him, he almost enjoyed having me suspect him. He took it for granted. I knew that he was playing around with other women. That's why I hired you. I wanted to find out who the latest was. Once, only once, we had a fight about it. We had a big scene and I cried a lot and he called me names and walked out of the apartment. He could never stand tears. He would walk out of the place and stay away for as long as he liked because he knew that I'd want him back just as soon as he cared to return. Then he would be all right for a while until he was ready for another adventure.'

'A charming arrangement,' I said. 'And you never knew any of these outside amours?'

She shook her head, numbly. 'I tried to follow him once. I went after him and actually followed him in a cab. But I couldn't follow through because I knew it wouldn't get me anywhere with him.' She twisted her handkerchief into a small knot. 'You see, I loved Michael.'

'So it could have been the blonde,' said Sybil.

'It could have been,' said Dolly. 'I never saw any of them. It might just as well have been that blonde!'

'You were worried about the blonde?'

She nodded again. 'I was worried about any good-looking woman he ever talked to.'

'Tell me what happened last night in your compartment.'

'Nothing happened. I was asleep. Michael had gone out and I was asleep.'

'You left before he returned?'

'I left when I found myself crying too hard. I had done it once before, a few months ago, and that time I fainted after a while. I didn't want him to find me in a faint, so I left the room.'

'How long after he was gone did you leave?'

'I don't know. I began to cry soon after he left. You can't keep track of time when you're upset like that. I decided I'd better get out and go to Sybil until I got over it.'

'Was that the only reason?'

She had stood up to get another drink. My question impeded her progress to the bottle. She stood there staring at me. Her face seemed paler now, almost a dead white.

'What do you mean by that?' she asked.

'Look,' I said, slowly. 'I mean what I mean. I figure you might have had another reason for getting out of that compartment. You might have had ideas, for instance. Maybe you were figuring on slapping your husband with the suitcase. Maybe you were afraid of what you might do to him if you were there when he returned.'

She backed slowly into the chair.

I decided to put it to her before the next paroxysm of woe had a head start.

I said, 'You were figuring on poisoning him?'

Her hand went to her throat in a reflex of surprise. She didn't answer.

Sybil got up and faced me, arms akimbo. 'For God's sake, Steve, what kind of stuff are you trying to pull? How in the world do you figure an angel like Dolly wanting to poison him?'

I said, 'I'm not bright enough to invent it, Sybil.' I reached into my pocket and brought out the little drugstore bottle. I walked across to Dolly and held it under her nose. She drew away from it as though it were a bottle of poison, which it was. She shrank into the chair and curled her legs under her and started to moan and cry in a higher crescendo.

'This,' I said, 'is a bottle of arsenic. Arsenic is a deadly poison, a pharmaceutical concoction used, occasionally, for murder! I found it in Dolly's luggage. I figured Dolly would rather have me hold it than the police. I also figured that if an autopsy showed that her husband was poisoned, this little bottle would do Dolly a lot of good at the bottom of the East River.'

Dolly came to her senses, quickly. 'He's right, Sybil — it is arsenic, but I swear I didn't use it! I had bought it to use, yes. I had decided that the very next time he left me for another woman I'd kill him. But I never used it!'

Sybil sank to the couch. 'Well, I'll be damned!'

I joined her. I pulled out my handkerchief and dabbed at my brow. I said, 'Play it again, Dolly — slower.'

'I didn't!' Dolly moaned. 'You've got to believe me! I loved him too much, I tell you. Sure, I hated him when he left me. He was always leaving me like that. He was always making a play for other women. But I didn't kill him! I couldn't kill Michael!'

I stared at the little bottle. I turned it over and over in my hand, feeling it, weighing it, rubbing it with my thumb. It was the usual pharmacy bottle, of light amber glass, narrow and ungrooved. I studied the liquid. I opened the cap and smelled it. I closed the cap and held it to the light. The bottle was filled almost full. It occurred to me, suddenly, that Dolly might be telling me the truth, and the truth left me cold, irritated me.

I said, 'I believe you. That makes everything just dandy. I came up here on the hook, frankly. I figured you all wrong, Dolly. But I've changed my mind.'

74

There was a silence, punctuated by the small clink of Sybil's glass being re-iced.

Dolly said, 'I'm glad you trust me. I hoped you would. Now you can forget all about that bottle and find out about what happened to Michael.'

'You want me to follow through?'

She smiled, for the first time. It lit her face and melted her eyes. She wasn't at all bad looking when she was happy. 'I've got plenty of money. If Michael was murdered, I'll spend it all to find out who did it.'

She was playing me straight now.

I said, 'Let me have some more of the background. Names and places. Friends and enemies.'

Dolly began to spill, slowly at first, but coherently and in a fine rhetoric. Michael had no close men friends. His women? She didn't know them by name or address. She had recognized them by the changes they wrought in Michael. When he was on the loose he was mean and moody and another character. She had grown used to his foibles. She knew that his affection moved in cycles. He was a good husband when he had dropped his 'other woman.' Dolly had accepted this formula until it brought on hysterics. It ate into her libido and transformed her into a weak and stupid wife, moved to tears when he abandoned her, joyful when he returned.

'What was his business?' I asked.

Dolly didn't know. He always had money — big money. He gave her as much as she needed. She spent all he gave her for a few years, and then began to bank most of her allowance money. It amounted to a goodly sum — and he had been heavily insured.

I said, 'You're giving me nothing at all. I can't go very far this way. Are you sure that you can't remember what he did for a living?'

'I never knew,' she told me. 'Michael always seemed to have money. I remember that he told me he was in the brokerage business just before we got married. I took his word for it. After all, did it matter?'

'It matters now. You're offering me only one trail — the trail that leads through his women. Yet, you don't know who these women were, do you?'

She shook her head.

Sybil said, 'Why don't you try your blonde girl friend, Detective?'

I got up smiling. I chucked Sybil under the chin. 'You want me to report back to you?'

'I'll be chewing my girdle waiting to hear from you.'

'You'll hear from me.'

I warned Dolly that she would be called by the police. I cautioned her to say nothing about the bottle of poison. I told her to let me know just as soon as anything happened. She offered me money, but I waved it away as though I didn't want it.

In the hall, I kissed Sybil good-bye.

She said, 'Next time you come visiting, make it for dinner.'

'When?'

'You should know,' Sybil said. 'You're the detective.'

7

Lester Henshaw greeted me in the city room at *The Courier*. He was a short, bird-like man, heavily lensed. He looked at you out of small, apprehensive eyes, flashing a broad and dirty-toothed smile. He was the movie type of newsman, too alert, too busy, and as friendly as a cordial pickpocket.

He kicked a seat over to me, took a cigarette from me and leaned over the desk on his elbows.

He said, 'All I know is what I read in the papers. Those atomic jerks are meeting at the International Hotel. They're on fire with their own importance, and who am I to blame them?'

'How long are they staying in town?'

Lester shrugged. 'It's a big deal. Something about forming an organization to prevent future wars. They want to throw their weight around in the halls of Congress. Some of them aren't too anxious for the publicity.' He jerked the cigarette out of his mouth and tipped the ashes on my pants. 'I shouldn't say that. I should say that most of them don't want to become public figures. They're hot from the dark closets of universities and classrooms.'

I said, 'How many of them are gathering?'

'Nothing but the upper strata. The gents at the International are the cream of nuclear physics.'

'How thick is the cream? There seemed to be a slew of them on the train the other night.'

He counted them out in his brain. 'Maybe a dozen of your fellow passengers were important. The rest were the usual hangers-on, assistants, staff people, and probably enough relatives to make the party festive.'

'Give them to me in the order of their importance, Lester.'

He gave them to me. The four old gentlemen in the news picture were the leaders. They were Cyril McCormack, Oscar Wyndham, John Frotti and Simon

Abelard. Three other minor bigshots were next: Albert Bruning, Theodore Evans, and George Reynolds. I pretended to be very much interested in these names. I badgered Lester for an hour, jotting small notes, asking small questions. Lester enjoyed all of this. He paused only to take my cigarettes and answer his phone.

He said, finally, 'You've got enough of this atomic guff to write a small book. What cooks?'

'I haven't begun to cook. How much have you got on any of these atomic gents?'

'You want to spend the week-end here? Maybe we'd better send out for blankets.'

I said, 'Let's break it down. Let's take the name Wyndham.'

'Oscar Wyndham?' Lester whistled an off-key note. 'We've got tons of crap on Oscar Wyndham. Oscar Wyndham was called in near the beginning. President Roosevelt — '

'Skip it. How about Mary Wyndham?'

I drew a blank. 'Who is she?'

'I asked you first. I met her on the train last night and she passed herself off as the old gent's niece.'

Lester buzzed a copy boy and sent him to the morgue. He returned with a few bushels of Wyndham matter. Lester tossed me an armful and I began to search through the stack for Mary.

Lester found her first.

He read me from a clipping: '*Mary Wyndham, a recent graduate of Vassar, has joined the staff of Oscar Wyndham, the eminent scientist. Miss Wyndham —* '

I tossed my clippings back across the desk. I said, 'That's enough. Now for Mr. Michael DePereyra.'

'Louder and funnier. Who in hell is he?'

I said, 'You've got a bad memory. DePereyra is the man who was found dead on that train.'

Lester gave me his professional squint, a facial manipulation halfway between a smile and a sneer. 'You begin to fascinate me, Steve. Unless these tired nostrils fail me, I detect the odor of a stew. I seem to smell two-and-two. What happens when you add them up?'

I gave him another cigarette and my boyish laughter. 'Let's start all over again,

Lester. What have you got about Michael DePereyra?'

He leaned far back in his chair and tucked his skinny hands behind his head. He made a great show of grinning at the window. He eyed the window in a lascivious way, as though the window was a naked woman. He half closed his eyes and continued to squint at the window, but the window hadn't been cleaned since 1938, when *The Courier* had bought out *The Blade*. I allowed him a minute to concentrate on the mud streaks.

After that, I stood up.

Lester swung away from his daydreams. 'Don't rush away, Steve! For God's sake, you can't blame a lush like me for trying to get on the inside of a story.'

'This story has no insides.'

'Rest your pants, Steve,' he pleaded. 'Let's keep this thing friendly.'

I didn't rest my pants. I said, 'Don't give me that routine. You ink maggots would kill your own grandmother for a by-line.'

Lester assumed a hurt expression. 'Not your old friend Lester. I admit I'm

82

aggressive. I admit I'm — '

I said, 'Why don't you admit you know nothing about DePereyra and we can go on from there?'

'All right. I don't know DePereyra. Nobody does if I don't. But I've got my own way of finding out things. You know that, Steve. If you'll only give me — '

I lit a cigarette and measured him for a coffin. 'I'll give you all the time in the world, chum. But I'll also bend back those big ears of yours and braid them behind your head if you so much as smell near the core of this thing. I don't want you near it, understand?'

He whistled again. 'It's that hot, eh? Well, you can count on old Lester to keep it mum until you give me the word.' He became very businesslike, suddenly. He jerked a pencil out of an ear and began to make hurried notes on a sheet of yellow paper. 'You figure an angle between DePereyra and Mary Wyndham?'

I leaned my full weight on his desk. I crumpled his yellow sheet of paper in one fist and tossed it over my shoulder. I brought my face up close to his, hardened it and opened it only wide enough to whisper: 'You and I, we're not talking about angles. We have no reason to link Mary Wyndham to anybody, do you follow me? We also have less reason for annoying Mary Wyndham. If we annoy Mary Wyndham in any way — even for a phony interview — we are liable to wake up one morning and find ourselves severely mutilated and in a convenient hospital. Are you listening, Lester?'

'I heard every word you said. You've got nothing to worry about, Steve.'

'Sure,' I said. 'That's exactly why I'm so worried.'

8

Mrs. Dunwoodie's place was four stories of brownstone, set neatly between two other houses of the same vintage. Mrs. Dunwoodie's house stood out on the street because of her decorative point of view. She had long ago decided to sandblast her establishment every five years. For this reason, her masonry was slick and colorful. Added to the neatness of the stonework was the woodwork, painted a deep blue on the windows and the big door on the street. Mrs. Dunwoodie was a fiend for decoration. Her garbage can, too, was tastefully smeared with the same deep blue. She prided herself on her curtains, always crisp and white and well ironed.

Mrs. Dunwoodie opened the door for me. She was a matronly woman, but the years sat well upon her solid hips. She had a sharp and shining face, still pretty enough to enjoy.

She was glad to see me. She led me into the living room, piloted me to the big soft chair, sat me in the chair and stood over me, beaming.

She brought me a drink, brought herself a drink and sat on the arm of my chair the way she always did with Max when she wanted to show him that she was the motherly type.

'Maxie, did he miss me?'

'Sure he missed you.' I patted her arm. 'What else?'

'I was wondering about Maxie. It's been lonely.'

'He'll be glad to hear about it.'

'Where is he?' she asked. 'He might have come here first. He knows — '

'He's out chasing a dame.'

She stiffened and busied herself with her drink. I felt like a heel playing games with Mrs. Dunwoodie.

'It's a case we think we've got,' I explained. 'Maxie has to chase a dame every time we get a case. You know that.'

'Another missing husband?'

'This one's missing for good. He was butchered on the train coming from

Chicago. I think.'

She made a funny sound, a bird noise, through her teeth. 'Isn't that too bad. That's a shame. And which dame is Maxie chasing, the widow?'

'You're knocking yourself out. Max never even saw the doll he's running after until I spotted her this morning down at the station.'

Mrs. Dunwoodie sighed. 'Oh, dear. All this probably means that Maxie will wear himself out again running around. He enjoys making a nervous wreck out of himself, that man. Who was killed?'

'Nobody. We've got very little on him. We're going to knock ourselves out getting a little more. We're working this one strictly from ten miles off the beam. We've got nothing — absolutely nothing.'

The phone rang and she picked it up anxiously, smiled into it, laughed into it and handed it over to me regretfully. 'It's Maxie,' she said.

Maxie was uptown, on Park Avenue, in the lobby of an apartment house. He was annoyed. He said: 'Her name is Brown — Gertrude Brown — and what I don't know about her is plenty.'

'Give me what you've got.'

'It's all written down,' Max said. 'She gave me plenty of nothing, like I said. She took a cab and got off at an office building on 45th Street. I followed her inside and I know that she went to the tenth floor and saw somebody in a dump called Butler Trading Company. She stayed inside for about half an hour and then waltzed out and took another cab and went downtown to a dirty neighborhood near the river. There was a big warehouse down there, also marked Butler Trading Company. It's a place right near the docks, a big black building somebody probably uses for a warehouse. Two floors, both dirty as the bottom of my shoe. She drifted inside this warehouse and stayed there for maybe fifteen, twenty minutes. This I couldn't understand. The warehouse is as lonely as a Canarsie cop, a funny place for a dame like her to be going.'

'You didn't go in?'

'What am I, a cloud of smoke?' Max grunted. 'Naturally I stayed on the outside. She came out, like I said, in about twenty minutes. I caught a good look at her walking into the cab. She looked worried this time. She looked really worried.'

'Neat guessing. Why did she look worried?'

'She was sort of running, for the first time. And her cab made a lot better time on the way uptown. I followed her over to a pawnshop on the Bowery. You'll never guess which one.'

I said, 'You make it tough. Was it Abe Mann's?'

'On the nose.'

'She went in for a gun?'

'I didn't wait to find out, but you can check with Abe. After all, it must have been a gun if she went to Abe's. Right?'

'Probably.' I made a note to call Abe Mann. 'How long did she stay in Abe's?'

'She did her business very quick,' Max said. 'Abe must have been waiting for her. Maybe somebody phoned him to have the gun ready?'

'That could be.'

'Abe might tell you. Anyhow, she ran

out of Abe's and went right up to Macy's. I followed her inside and she ran me ragged. I figured maybe she was wise to me tailing her and was trying to shake me in Macy's.'

'She shopped?'

'She didn't shop. She ran. She kept walking fast through the place, as if she was looking for something. She left the place on the Broadway side and beat it down the subway. That was where I figured she really must have been wise to me tailing her. A doll like Gertrude Brown don't usually go slumming in subways. She got out fast — at 49th Street, walked through Radio City to Fifth Avenue and then hopped another cab. She wound up where she is now, in this floozy apartment across the street.'

'Her own apartment?'

'That's what the doorman says. Also the elevator boy.'

'Is that all you could get from them?'

'What did you expect in ten minutes — the key to her apartment? I can get more from the elevator boy. He has a nose for dollar bills. But I figured I better not rush it otherwise he might tell the dame about me. Am I smart?'

'A genius,' I said. 'You know her apartment number?'

'She hangs out in apartment 1011.'

'Stay with her. If she doesn't leave her apartment by ten o'clock, come back. I'll be here at that time.'

Max didn't want to stop talking. 'Where have you been, Steve?'

I said, 'Sybil Drake's. We're working, Max. I'm on my way out. Stay where you are. I need you there. You're earning dough for us right where you are.'

I went upstairs to my room. I took a shave and a shower and changed my tie and shirt. For some reason or other I moved with a sudden urgency. It seemed to me that I would have to ask a lot of questions soon — and that some of these questions would remain unanswered. I charted a simple course, laying out the important stops in my new routine. Louis Jennick and Abe Mann and Gertrude Brown headed my list.

I brought the name of Abe Mann to the

top, took a cab and started for the Bowery.

Abe Mann's emporium was a dirty storefront in a dirty building three blocks from the entrance to the Manhattan Bridge. It was an unlovely façade, wedged between a grim building bearing the sign:

EMPIRE STATE HOTEL
Rooms For Men
25 cents

and another, dirtier building as inviting as the entrance to a cemetery.

Abe had thrived at his maggoty trade for over thirty years, and all of these years were worked behind the ancient gray-glass front. The decaying gold-lettered word: LOANS was the only decoration on the glass. Overhead, the symbolic three-balled trade mark swung lazily in the downtown breeze.

I opened the door and a small bell rang from deep inside the clutter of merchandise. Abe himself stepped out of the shadows and peered at me from over his big lenses. He was a neat character, clean and white around the shirt and collar. He had a face out of Dickens, wrinkled and lean and adorned by a large wart, high on his right cheek. His eyes were small and blue and bright as the highlights on his spectacles. He greeted me with a fine show of business affection. I shook his hand and his grip was thirty years younger than his face.

I said, 'It's been a long time, Abe.'

His voice still held the professorial overtones that had made him famous and infamous.

'You are down here seeking information, eh, Ericson?'

'You're still a good man at guessing games, Abe.'

He waved it away into the shadows. 'Nonsense. Detectives have a glow of their own. I've seen it too often in the past to mistake it for anything but curiosity — of a professional nature.'

I said, 'Interesting. How's business, Abe?'

He looked at me over his glasses and smiled. His smile was brittle and knowing and went well with his eyes. He leaned on his bony hands and tapped the longest finger of his right hand.

He said, 'Get to it. What do you want to know?'

'Do you still sell guns?'

'Very rarely.'

'Is today one of your rare days?'

'You want a gun?'

I shook my head. 'I have a gun. Every private eye is allowed one gun and one brain.'

'Some,' said Abe, 'have only the gun. You have both.'

'Thanks. You sold a gun this morning?'

'I might have.'

'You might have sold it to a woman?'

He nodded, closing his eyes on the downbeat. 'That is highly possible.'

'Who was she?'

'I never ask my customers foolish questions.'

I took out my wallet and flipped it open, slowly. I reached into it and removed two five-dollar bills. I laid the two bills on the counter and disregarded them. I said, 'Who was she?'

Abe picked up the bills and folded them neatly into a small bundle. He caressed the bundle with his fingertips and then slid it across the counter until it touched my hand.

'I really don't know, Ericson.'

'Would you know for twenty?'

'I wouldn't know for a hundred and twenty.'

'What make did she buy?'

'It might have been a Colt.'

'A loaded Colt?'

Abe shrugged. 'I never examine firearms. They make me feel very uncomfortable. I sell them just as I find them back on the shelf.'

'This woman,' I said. 'Was she an old customer?'

'I've never seen her before.'

'She was sent here?'

'I've never seen her before,' he repeated. 'So far as I know, she walked in off the street.'

'A high-class transient,' I said.

'A high-class transient.'

We weren't getting anywhere and were taking our time about it. I gave him a cigarette, lit it for him and waited for him to exhale.

I said, 'This thing is bigger than just a gun and a pretty dame, Abe. It might pay you to keep your nose clean.'

He examined his cigarette with great care, searching for something very important in the lit end. He took another drag, a slow one, and watched the smoke float away over his head.

'The police, Ericson?'

'Maybe. A lot depends on some ideas I have. But if the little woman in the leopard coat was sent here, I ought to know who sent her.'

Abe ground out the cigarette on the counter, shaking his head in rhythm with the grinding.

'I'm an honest man, Ericson. She walked in off the street. Out of a taxicab.'

I picked up the bills on the counter and stuffed them into my wallet. I said: 'You're covering for somebody, Abe. That's your affair. You did it once before, a long time ago, and got yourself in a jam. You remember?'

'I remember.'

'This jam may be bigger. This jam may be big enough to put you away for a while. If Heath gets wind of this — and he might — he'll be down here sweating the information out of you. You don't have to worry about me, Abe. You know that. Your biggest worry is the little dame in the leopard coat and the little Colt she's got in her handbag. Maybe she just wants it to scare her friends. Maybe she collects guns. But if she ever drills anybody with that firing piece, the smell will lead straight to your door and then you may be sorry.'

He was watching me as I talked. You had the feeling that he was doing intricate mathematical calculations as he watched you. His little eyes drilled into yours and found the soft spot behind them, nearest the brain. He looked at me and all the way through me into my motive and my character and the inner gears of my brain.

I turned on my heel and started for the door.

He stopped me when my hand was on the knob. He said: 'It might be that she was sent here.'

'By whom?' I asked, still at the door.

'Nobody.' He was serious now. He was trying to sell me his earnestness. 'Do you understand, Ericson? Nobody called me to tell me she was coming. But she might have been sent here, all the same. She's been down here before.'

'You mean she's been here with somebody?'

'Precisely.'

I got back to the counter quickly. 'How long ago, and with whom?'

'She was here about two months ago, with a man. That man might have sent her down here this morning.'

'What man?'

'I don't know his name.'

'I'm beginning to believe you,' I said. 'Let me describe him for you, Abe. He was a tall gent, good looking, and as smooth and slick as a pants ad in *Esquire*. He spoke through his nose, in the phony English school of dialogue. He had the type of breeding that smells from *Town and Country* mixed with stale beer and pastrami. He walked in cocky, got what he wanted and then left you feeling that he had done you a big favor. Maybe you don't know his name. You don't have to know his name, Abe. You'd remember him because you've got a head for remembering his type of character. Or am I talking to myself?'

Abe smiled his thin and weary smile. 'You've got him, Steve. And I don't know his name. A friend of yours?'

'A casual acquaintance,' I said. 'A five-minute friend.'

'You looking for him?'

'I know where he is, Abe. He's laying on a slab down at the morgue, as cold as a piece of herring in a Greek salad!'

9

I slept late the next day. When my eyes opened, they opened without my brain, so I hugged the bed and explored the pillow for more angles. I found nothing but confusion while awake, so I closed my eyes again and abandoned my brain.

I went down for Mrs. Dunwoodie's supper and after supper relaxed in the living room. I sprawled on the couch, munching the tasty remains of a turkey sandwich, fondling the cold neck of a beer bottle, and wondered whether a real homicide dick operated with any more system than my scatterbrained routine. I figured any police dick would know a lot more than I did about poisons and autopsies and the thousand and one details of butchering for fun and profit.

I also figured that most city dicks I knew were mighty smart about certain things and mighty stupid about others. I decided, finally, that if they were smarter it was because they worked in groups, like fat hounds after a sly fox. I concluded that they were, therefore, a bunch of halfwits.

I looked at my watch and then telephoned Louis Jennick, my friend who made a meager living as janitor down at the morgue. I asked him questions about the stiff tagged M. DePereyra.

He said: 'They just finished with your handsome boy friend, Steve.'

'What killed him?'

'Nothing killed him. He just died.'

I blew an impatient snort into the mouthpiece. 'That's impossible! You mean they didn't find anything suspicious?'

Louis Jennick laughed. 'Look, Steve, nothing is impossible in a place like this. A stiff comes in. They cut it up. They make up their minds what killed it. They make up their minds slow and careful like — not like a certain private eye I know. The docs get together and cut. They fiddle around plenty with the insides of a dead man before they hand out news, you follow me?'

I said, 'Then he wasn't poisoned?'

'All I know is what I hear. They just left here, a few minutes ago. They tell me he died from natural causes, like maybe a weak ticker. They don't mention a word about any poison.'

I thanked him and hung up. I lit a cigarette and loosened my collar and sat there smoking and staring out of the window. Outside, it was as black and empty as my head.

A half hour later Max came in. He wasn't happy. His eyes were bagged and tired looking. He threw his hat in the corner, followed by his coat and dropped himself into the soft seat near the couch.

I said: 'Did she leave last night?'

Max scowled up at me. 'She stayed home last night. She also stayed home all day. I got up there again early this morning and watched the apartment lobby all day. Your leopard lady is still inside. She didn't leave the place since yesterday.'

'Anybody visiting with her?'

'Ask me something easy. I didn't get that friendly with the elevator boy. You think she's entertaining? And suppose she is? Who the hell is she and why should we give a damn?'

I said: 'She's Gertrude Brown and she took a fit when she saw DePereyra's wife yesterday morning. She also visited the Butler Trading Company, probably looking for somebody she couldn't find. Then she went up to Abe Mann's and bought herself a Colt.'

Max sat up, alive again. 'I thought so.'

'There's more. Abe Mann told me that she was in his place some time ago. With a gentleman friend.'

'That I don't follow,' Max said wearily.

'You will when I tell you that Gertrude's friend was our boy — Michael DePereyra.'

That brought Max to his feet and opened his mouth again. 'Slower and easier, Steve. I'm away down in the cellar, digging for mushrooms, while all the time you're up in the attic. I'm up at Park Avenue watching a doorman until I can tell you how many stitches there are in the cuffs of his pants. I don't get the connection between Gertrude Brown and this DePereyra fish. Where do we fit?'

I told him how we fit. I began at the beginning, including the bottle of poison, and brought him up to date. Max listened attentively, as he always did when facts were forthcoming. He was counting out the facts and sorting them in the small storehouses of his brain. He was sifting them and filing them, but not theorizing about them. Max was not a man for promoting theories.

He let me finish and then said: 'All of that stuff is very interesting, especially the autopsy. I am just tired enough to get dizzy from so much stuff. I'm also tired enough to ask you what we can do about it.'

I put on my jacket and straightened my collar and tie. 'You take yourself a nap, Maxie. Mrs. Dunwoodie will be back from the movies soon and she'll make you some strong coffee. When I get back from where I'm going you may need it.'

'Where are you going?'

'I'm visiting. I'm taking a cab uptown to Park Avenue for a short chat with Gertrude Brown.'

'She may have company now.'

I got my shoulder holster out of the closet. It was my small holster, the one with the Colt .38 automatic in it. I strapped it on and slid into my topcoat.

At the doors I said, 'It might be fun to meet some of Gertrude's friends. Maybe I'll be lucky enough to meet Mr. Somebody from the Butler Trading Company.'

'You're not talking sense, Steve.' Max made a face at me. 'If you want in up there, remember, the elevator boy twitches when he sees a dollar bill. He'll probably float if you give him a fin.'

'I'll remember that,' I said and went out.

10

Gertrude Brown lived in the lush core of Park Avenue, the money-belt region just north of 60th Street, the land of clean sidewalks and small dogs and festooned doormen and well-furred women who held themselves high and walked as though they knew you stared at them. And you usually did.

It was after eleven when I paid off my cabbie and entered the marble front of the big apartment house. The doorman was off duty, so I pushed the revolving door myself. The lobby was big enough for a small convention. It was designed to feature the glowing dignity of a white statue in a light blue fountain. The statue wasn't worth it. It was an elf, astride a small deer, who seemed hell-bent on throwing himself into a dither because a small frog sat on the rock beneath him.

I stared at the fountain. I stared at

the elbow of the elf, so that I was able to include the face and shoulders of the elevator boy beyond the elbow. He stood in the door of his elevator, chewing a toothpick. He was a small youth, of the pimply-faced variety. He had a face full of nose and cheek, but his mother had forgotten to put a chin under his nose. His eyes flitted to the statue, slyly, speculatively, estimating my importance in a roundabout sort of way.

I abandoned the fountain and entered the elevator. He closed the door and kept his back to me, saying nothing.

I handed him a five-dollar bill, neatly folded so that the numeral glared at him. I said: 'Tenth floor.'

He made a big show of studying the bill. The toothpick dropped out of his mouth, and his little eyes tried for composure, but the five was too much for him.

He said: 'I can't do this. I'm supposed to announce you, mister.'

'Sure you are. Forget it. There'll be another fin for you when I come down.'

'How do I know when you're coming down?'

'I'll be down. I can't fly.'

He pressed the lever and we went up, fast. When he opened the door for me, he said: 'If you stay too long, I won't be here when you come out. I go off duty soon.'

I took out my wallet and played with it, allowing him to estimate the greenness of it. I pinched out another five and let it hang in my hand.

I said: 'Is she alone?'

He didn't take his eyes off my wallet. 'She should be. I didn't see anybody come in.'

I handed him the five and walked down the hall on the yellow carpet. There were three doors on the floor and number 1011 was farthest from the elevator. I hesitated at 1011 until I heard the elevator start down. Then I rang the bell.

From inside came the sound of a musical gong. It rang three times, on three notes, like commercial radio chimes.

Gertrude Brown opened the door for

me. She didn't seem at all surprised to see me.

Up close, she was a striking woman. She had on a green pajama suit, flared around the hips and cut low to promote her chest appeal. Her hair was as black as a raven's overcoat, parted in the middle and dropping in provocative swirls around her fine shoulders. She had a surly mouth, a red pout. Her black eyes assessed me as lazily as a cobra focusing on a rabbit.

She said: 'Yes?' as though she were answering the telephone. It was a meaningful word, complete with arched eyebrows and the deadpan look expert housewives save for brush salesmen.

I said: 'May I come in?'

'By all means,' she said. 'I expected you sooner.'

I stepped into a squarish foyer, done in greens and grays. It was a cold room, too cold for comfort. In a wall mirror, a white face stared at me. I swallowed hard, because the face was mine.

She didn't offer to take my hat and coat. She swept a hand in the direction of the living room, then glided in ahead of me.

In the living room, a man was waiting for me. He sat at the far end of the room, against a background of silver draperies. He sat in a big chair. He was bigger than the chair. He leaned back comfortably and smiled at me. His smile was only a small part of his fat face. I didn't watch his face for long. I was watching his right hand.

His right hand held a gun. He waved it toward the couch.

He said, pleasantly: 'Sit down, my friend. Sit down.'

I sat. Gertrude Brown stood near the fat man. She said: 'I told you he would come. The other one was only the tail.'

The man in the chair continued to smile. He was a big boy, big all over. He had the type of frame that was all lard and muscle and undisguised power. He had big hands, hamlike and hairy and made to order for mayhem. His head was fringed with gray, curled around the ears and neck in the manner of a violin virtuoso, or the careless trim of an artist.

His face shone with a Santa Claus glow, the pinkness of it accented by the gray eyebrows. He had sharp blue eyes, as cold as the back of my spine. He was dressed well. He sported a pinstripe suit of dark blue and gray, a white shirt and a violent tie that made his ample chest a resting place for a lavish design of flowers and bees and other assorted tie-maker follies. He looked like somebody's grandfather playing with a toy pistol. And a toy detective.

'Your friend,' he began. 'Why didn't you bring him with you?'

'I don't have any friends,' I said.

His little mouth curled slightly and I caught a tic high on his right cheekbone. It made his right eye wink. He moved his massive head gently and aimed it Gertrude's way.

He said, 'He doesn't have any friends.'

Gertrude Brown said, 'He's a god-damned liar!'

'Oh, no,' I said. 'I hate people. I really do.'

The fat man attempted a chuckle but didn't strain too much to make it heard.

When it died away he was still staring at me with his lip curled, and the right eye was winking in an unrefined way.

'A droll fellow,' he said to Gertrude, waving my way with the little toy pistol. 'A man with a sense of humor.'

Gertrude Brown didn't smile. She stood there, against the wall, her arms crossed over her ample curves. She stared at me with a fixed and unwavering stare. She was registering hate and doing a fine job of it.

The fat man said, 'A man with an assistant who follows people about can be only one of two things.' He surveyed the ceiling and gave it his dialogue. 'He can be either a blackmailer or a detective.'

He was well pleased with himself. He opened his eyes wide and his eyebrows lifted and his little mouth smiled and he sat that way until his right eye winked twice, slowly.

I said, 'You're knocking yourself out, fat man. An assistant doesn't mean a thing these days. A man with an assistant who follows people could be lots of things. He could be a murderer. He could also be a process server.'

'Clever. Quite clever. But you are a detective.'

'Tell me more.'

Gertrude Brown moved restlessly behind me. I heard a small metallic click and then smelled cigarette smoke.

The fat man pursed his lips and closed his eyes. When he opened them all the humor had gone. His pudgy hand held the gun steady on his knee.

'It is too bad that you are a detective,' he said. 'What is your name?'

'My name is Phineas Q. Flabbingnagle,' I said. 'Of the Flabbingnagle Detective Service. I specialize in lost dogs and babysitting. I was on my way to a babysitting session and picked the wrong apartment. It happens to the best of detectives.'

Gertrude Brown stirred restlessly behind me. 'Stop playing games with him!' she said. 'His jokes are killing me.'

The big man said, 'Patience, my dear. Your assistant, young man, isn't very well trained. I'd discharge him, if I were you. He was seen.'

'I fired him,' I said. 'I just put a down payment on a beagle.'

The fat man placed the gun on the chair arm and reached into his massive jacket. He lit the cigarette slowly, making a great show of nonchalance, punctuated by a few winks from his dirty right eye. The holster under my arm began to hum and I itched to show my gun to them. But I decided against it. The fat man would have liked me to display my firearms.

'And you instructed your assistant to follow Miss Brown about. You approached her in Grand Central Station and then set your man on her.'

He was a schoolteacher, reciting facts and waiting for the classroom nod.

I nodded. 'You, too, are a detective.'

'Thank you. If I were a detective, I would be a good one. A good detective does not show his hand until he has filled it with aces. At the present moment I must withhold judgment of your abilities. You have made several mistakes, my friend. You have started with a mistake and then made it worse by acting without thought. An expert would have thought twice before coming up here.'

'How right you are,' I said. 'I'm such a silly boy. I'm just silly enough to want to spit in your eye.'

He chuckled at that one. It was a brief chuckle, ending suddenly in a petulant frown.

'Why are you following Miss Brown?' he asked.

'Her coat. I'm a pervert about leopard coats.'

He didn't register humor on that one. He motioned to Gertrude and she stepped over to him. He said: 'Take his gun away!'

She came over to me, stiffly. The big man froze. He leaned toward me in the chair and I saw his fat knuckles go white on the trigger. It was no time for horseplay.

So I tried horseplay. When she pulled at my jacket, I grabbed her around the waist and held her there, her back to him. Her arms came up to my face, trying for my eyes. I felt a fingernail dig into my right cheek and pulled at her arm. She was strong, far too strong for a woman of her size.

The fat man rose from his chair and was across the room in a few quick movements. Gertrude and I were locked in a mad embrace. Her hands were in my hair now, but I paid them no mind. My good, free hand was almost at my holster.

My fingers were touching the leather of the holster when the blow came. The fat boy hit me from behind, a swift, hard crack that stopped all movement, and sent me to my knees in a heap. There was a loud buzzing in the room and a light haze settled around my ears.

Over the hum I heard her say: 'Hit him again, the bastard!'

But he didn't hit me again. His big arm swept me into a chair. He jerked the gun out of my holster and pocketed it. He leaned over me and slapped my face with a palm as wide as a baked ham. And twice as hard.

Then he stood back and laughed at me. I looked up at him and there were three of him and behind the three fat men, three women, swaying and bending in a nightmare of diffused light. I wanted to get up and wade into the six of them. I wanted to bring those images back into focus and then murder them.

So I sat there, swaying and shaking and muttering feeble dialogue to my inner man. They allowed me to sit for a while. I sat and shook until the room came into focus again and the fat man was back in his chair at the end of the room, all in one piece and still holding the little black gun.

'Now then,' he said, as though we had just stopped our talk for a sip of a highball. 'Now then, my good detective, perhaps you will tell me why you were following Miss Brown.'

I didn't answer. I played it dumb and groggy, allowing my head to roll a bit. I let the silence build to nothing.

Gertrude said, 'Maybe you'd better hit him again.'

'I don't think so, my dear,' said the fat man. 'He'll talk to me very soon. We must give him a bit of time, mustn't we, my good detective?'

'Go to hell!' I said.

The fat man clucked, sadly. He got out

of his chair and came over to me. He hit me with the baked ham again, hard enough to send the light out of my brain. I sagged and bit into my lip, hard. I didn't want to faint. I let myself lean with his blow and came down heavily on the arm of the chair. My head was on an oiled hinge. The hinge had swung downward, toward my chest. There was no mechanism for raising the hinge so that my head could be lifted back to normal. There was a small switch somewhere in the back of my mind, but it was beyond my grasp — I couldn't reach it with my muscles.

I heard his voice again, after a while.

He was saying, 'You had your man follow Miss Brown. Why?'

The silence was short.

'You had your man follow her from Grand Central Station. Why?'

My mouth opened, just wide enough to inhale. I couldn't have answered if I had wanted to. And I didn't want to. His face was close to mine. I felt his breath in my ear. He was shouting now. His voice, through the mist, was heavier and carried a vibration befitting his bulk.

'Why did you have her followed? Somebody hired you! Who? Who hired you to follow Miss Brown? Who?'

From somewhere in Brooklyn came the voice of Gertrude Brown. It was a high whisper, loaded with venom. 'He won't talk, the stupid jerk!'

'He'll talk. I'll persuade him.'

'He's not the type. He's been seeing too many movies.'

'Give him time. He'll talk.'

'Not a chance. He's a Boy Scout. He'll sit there and let you massage his face all night. Maybe we'd better get him out of here.'

'Not yet.'

I felt the fat man's fist clutching my shirt. He dragged me upright. He shook me until the hinge began to squeal. He kept shaking my head with quiet desperation. It was winding him.

My mouth opened and I found myself unable to close it.

He didn't give up the shaking. I was on a merry-go-round — a small, soundless merry-go-round that travelled in a small circle at breakneck speed. I was whirling off into space, flying into the clouds, big gray clouds, then red clouds and finally black clouds filled with the hum of mad internal music.

Then I was out.

11

Something cold and wet hit me in the face and I woke up. The coldness and wetness was water and the water was all over my face and hair. The man who had spilled it over me was laughing at me and I recognized his laughter.

It was the fat man. He stood away from me, in the center of the rug. He held a glass in his left hand and a cigarette in his right hand and just stood there bubbling with laughter. He had dainty gestures. He moved over to the small table near the couch and placed the empty glass on it tenderly and noiselessly.

Gertrude Brown was not in the room. I missed her. For some reason or other I felt safer with the woman around. There is something about a woman, even a bad woman that lends respectability and normalcy to any situation. A woman doesn't like the sight of blood. A woman might jump at the sound of a gun. Killing would be a lot easier with Gertrude out of the room.

'You are wondering about Miss Brown,' said my fat friend, as smugly as though he had read my mind. Which he had. 'Miss Brown is gone, and you're wondering what will happen now.'

He had the annoying habit of stating a theory as a fact.

I said, 'I'm wondering how soon I'll be able to walk over and spit in your eye.'

'Oh, come now,' he said, merrily. 'Let's forget about the past. We can be friends if you'll only curb your evil temper.'

'I'm fussy about my friends. I don't go in for fat slobs.'

'Pish! There you go again. Your temper will be your ruination, my good detective friend. It doesn't pay a private investigator to fly off the proverbial handle the way you do. I can make your time valuable if you will cooperate.' He sat down.

He wanted me to answer, so I kept my mouth shut.

'I know that you were following Miss Brown, obviously. I also know that you have a friend, a partner, who kept after

122

her all day. Why?'

I continued my silence. I studied the carpet carefully, taking in the design, the edge of the carpet and the chair he was sitting in. My contemplation of the rug included a brief survey of his gun. He still held it on his knee, a big boy with a lollypop.

'You told Miss Brown that you were sent to the train to meet another young woman. Your explanation was obviously false. You used it only as a means for meeting Miss Brown. Why?'

'I like dames. I'm funny that way.'

The telephone rang from somewhere, a muffled ring. The fat man sighed and stood up. He eyed me for a flicker of a moment, measuring my capacities. Then, holding the gun stiffly at his side, he walked toward a small cabinet at the window, five feet away.

'Hello,' he said. 'No, he is still here. He will probably be here for quite a while. You will remain away until I call you.'

He turned for an instant to replace the receiver. It was in that instant that I made up my mind. I threw myself at him blindly, aiming for his paunch. I dove for him and hit him exactly where I had hoped to hit him. My shoulder struck hard, hard enough to send him tail over teacups against the cabinet. I heard him blow air in a reflex of surprise and shock. His body was just as hard as I thought it would be. We went down together, the mountain and the molehill.

I hit him three or four times again, low and dirty. I pounded his paunch until my fist ached and I heard him moan. We were on the floor and I kept him there. My fist hammered into his jaw until I got tired of the exercise. Then I began to slap his face the way he had slapped mine.

But it was all very silly. I had put him away with the first few belly punches. I was making an ass of myself. So I slapped him again across his fat face and then stood up.

I walked over to the cabinet and poured myself a full hooker of Bourbon. I downed it and three others in quick succession. The apartment was quiet. The noise of my own movements irritated me. Everything else about the place irritated me. I decided that my head was hurting and I had better move quickly. I was hungry for fresh air.

I returned to the fat man. He lay on his side, one arm outstretched, the other bent under him. His face, in repose, was cherubic. His small mouth pouted petulantly, and a thin stream of blood trickled to his chin and under his chin to his collar.

I opened his jacket. He was sporting an alligator wallet of the imported type. He had a thousand dollars or so in fifty and hundred dollar bills. In the cellophane window of the wallet there was a photograph of a woman. She was a young woman, as young as Gertrude Brown, but not as striking.

There were six business cards in one of the folds. They were deluxe, these cards, engraved on a fine, slick, thinnish sort of paper. All six of them read:

Hiram Goodson
The International Hotel

I pocketed one of these cards and

continued my quick frisk. His jacket pockets interested me. Hiram Goodson smoked Turkish cigarettes. He had a box of paper matches marked 'Pan American Airways.' And in his inside pocket I found an interesting item. It was a newspaper clipping, a photo — ripped from a paper and not cut. I recognized the type — the clipping came from a city tabloid:

FOUR ATOMIC SCIENTISTS
TO CONFER
McCormack, Wyndham, Frotti and Abelard arrive at Grand Central Station for forthcoming meeting of renowned experts.

I folded the clipping into my wallet and then stood there slapping the wallet against my palm. I began to laugh at myself. I called myself a few names and returned the clipping to Hiram Goodson's jacket.

I moved into the kitchen, a trim and highly polished food den that smelled only from cleanliness. There were no crumbs on the smooth work board. The icebox carried only a few trays of ice cubes and a half-dozen bottles of ginger ale and soda. There was no food.

Gertrude Brown's bedroom intrigued me. It was a large room, done in the severely modern style of decoration. A huge bed sat on a heavy, white rug. The bed was low and soft and large enough for a five-handed game of poker, with room for kibitzers. There was a galaxy of pillows and cushions. A small night table held a bright, modern lamp and a copy of *Forever Amber*. Near that bed it looked good.

I opened the drawers of a severe, blonde chest, loaded with feminine undergarments. Gertrude Brown's closet was loaded with many dresses, coats, shoes and hats. But on the top shelf, a metallic highlight attracted me. I pulled it down.

It was a framed picture — a photograph. It was a picture of Michael DePereyra, smiling an even-toothed smile into the camera. On the bottom, inked in white, was the message:

To Helena — with love from Michael

In the living room, my fat friend slept peacefully. I relieved him of my automatic and returned it to my holster. I found his gun where it had fallen, near the small cabinet. I removed the shells, dropped them into a potted plant on the window ledge, and pocketed the gun. I walked into the kitchen and drank a tall glass of water. I wiped off the glass and stood there shaking my head and cursing Gertrude Brown. I cursed her for her neatness and her polished kitchen and the lack of information in her delightful nest.

I strolled back to examine my fat friend. He lay in the same position, a fallen Santa Claus asleep and snoring gently. He had stopped bleeding. I stood there in the silence, fixing his face and figure in my memory. The sight of him disturbed me. The quiet crept into my brain and pounded against my ears, throbbed with the rhythm of my pulse reminding me that my head had been hit recently.

The sudden ringing of the telephone

knifed the silence and made my stomach dance. I lifted the receiver and heard a woman's voice say: 'Hello?'

The voice was deep enough and rich enough to belong to Gertrude Brown. I said nothing. I put the receiver down and wiped it with my handkerchief and let her talk to the table top. She said: 'Hello?' again, this time higher and louder.

I got my hat and coat and left the place. The elevator boy had aged considerably. He no longer had a weak chin and a pimply face. Now he was an old man, with a graying mustache and watery eyes. These eyes reflected terror when he assessed my well-mauled face.

I said, 'What happened to your son?'

'My son?'

'The little stinker who took me up a little while ago — where is he?'

The old man shook his head, slowly. 'You mean Arthur. Arthur went home, all of a sudden. I don't know why. They called me to take his shift.'

'He won't be back,' I said.

12

The lobby was dark, but the elf on the deer could still look down at the frog because a small bulb glowed in the frog's mouth. I crossed the hall and found a phone booth hidden in the shadows.

I dialed Police Headquarters.

I said: 'You'd better send a couple of men up to Gertrude Brown's apartment, in the Shropshire House on Park Avenue. The apartment number is 1011. A man has been murdered. It's ghastly.'

I hung up and walked through the revolving doors and the cold air hit me and braced me. A man approached me from the north and fell in with my stride.

He said: 'It's about time. I was just about to lam up there and pull you out.'

I kept walking. I said, 'Okay, Maxie. You're a sweetheart. I'm all right, but a certain fat slob upstairs is flat on his fanny.'

'Who?'

'You don't know him. He was a big boy named Goodson and he had a fine time slapping me around, first with a little gun and then with a very large fist. He seemed worried about what we were doing. Wanted to know more about us. I told him plenty of nothing. So he hit me until I couldn't breathe. After that it was my turn. I dove for his pot and made it. I left him up there on the floor.'

'The girl, too?'

'I don't hit dames that way. Anyhow, she wasn't around. She faded after the first round.'

'I don't get it,' said Max. 'Who is this Goodson?'

'That's what we're going to find out. I just phoned the police.'

Max jerked to a stop. 'Hit me easier, Steve. This fat boy must have sapped the brain out of you. Why the police?'

'Why not? He's doing us no good on his larded can up in Gertie's flat. Where would it get us to let him sleep up there all night?'

'Where does it get us to move him out of there?'

131

I continued our slow walk. 'You know the gentleman?'

'All I know is what I read in your baby-blue eyes. His name is Goodson. What else?'

'His name is plenty. You remember the notes I found in DePereyra's pocket?'

Max showed me the corners of his mouth. 'You never let me see any notes.'

I said: 'DePereyra's notes referred to a Mr. 'G.' He also made reference to contacting 'B.' soon. And the telegram mentioned Butler. Does it begin to sound off in your dome?'

'It helps. 'G.' is Goodson. 'B.' is Gertie Brown. And Butler is the office. So what else?'

'Nothing else. That's why I wanted to smoke the bastard out of there. All we have is his name and a good guess at his weight. He's a fat man named Goodson. Is he the guy she was looking for in the Butler Trading Company? Is he an uncle of hers, in the city for the laughs? Maybe he's a rich sugar merchant who's keeping her in marshmallows and furs. Maybe he's her father, or her brother. How do we know? We don't know. So we call the police and put him on the spot. If he's the type I think he is, our fat Goodson will spurn police. He'll waddle out of that place and head somewhere. When that happens, a little man with a sad pan will be waiting for him. The little man with the sourpuss will hang back and tail him.'

Max chuckled. 'How long does this go on?'

'Until he beds down his fat pants.'

We had walked five blocks from Gertrude Brown's place. From over on Lexington Avenue came the thin wail of a squad car siren.

'They're fast, when it isn't important,' said Max, and turned on his heel to start back.

I said, 'Be careful, Maxie. No loose ends this time. Keep your distance and never let him know you're there. Don't show yourself. I'll meet you back at the rat nest.'

I took a cab to Reuben's. I ordered a big pot of coffee and a Hildegarde sandwich and sat there munching Hilde- garde and gulping the coffee and scribbling foolish messages to myself on the back of a small index card. It was an old habit of mine, this whistling in the dark on paper. My pencil skipped nimbly all over the small card, but my brain was far from Reuben's. My brain was actively concerned with the occasional thumps of pain from a hot lump behind my ear and a dark woman with nice hips and a bad temper. And a man named Goodson.

I kept writing absolutely nothing at all and thinking twice as much. There was the business of the clipping in Goodson's pocket, the scrap of newsprint with the pictures of four atomic scientists on it. I went over their names: McCormack, Wyndham, Frotti and Abelard. I crossed out McCormack and Frotti and Abelard. That left Wyndham. I held Wyndham in my mind and on the paper. I printed his name in large, black letters. I drew a ragged circle around his name and stared at it. The name meant nothing to me but the pretty face and figure of Mary Wyndham and the way she shook my hand and looked into my eyes and made sport of my profession.

I drew a long black arrow from the circled name to the edge of the card. At the edge I printed the name Goodson. Why had Goodson kept a clipping of this type? I put down the pencil and sat back to laugh at myself. Millions of people must have clipped news items about the atomic masterpiece that rocked the world. Goodson was intelligent enough to be interested in atomic energy and atomic scientists.

I dug my pencil into both names and slowly blacked them out. I tore the index card into very small pieces, pulled out another one and recommenced my mental meanderings. I thought of the small black gun in Goodson's larded fist. It was a big fist and a small gun, a stupid, feminine gun for a man of his size. He had handled it gingerly, but well. He had held it with the air of a man long used to guns of all types and sizes. But the gun — was it his? A gun that size would fit neatly into a midget's hip pocket, or the overstuffed handbag that Gertrude Brown had carried. It was a fine fowling piece for a hard-boiled wench like Gertie.

I reached into my pocket and fingered the cold steel of the little gun. The coldness of it crept up my fingers and into my arm and over my shoulder until it hit my spine. I withdrew my hand.

When I looked up, a tall man in a sport coat stood near the cashier's desk, staring inside. He saw me before I had noticed him. He came toward me taking long strides and smiling a broad smile. It was Professor McCormack.

I shook his hand and waved him to a seat. He seemed overjoyed to see me again, sorry that I had already finished.

I said, 'Do all scientists spend the early hours looking for salami and eggs?'

He was a gentle man with a gentle laugh. He used it almost obligingly, in the way a parent laughs at a child's joke.

'Scientists are human beings,' he said. 'This is my favorite spot for a snack.'

'You're a New Yorker?'

'Oh, no. You don't usually find New Yorkers in a place like this. These celebrated places are in business for people like me, Ericson. They exist only because somebody from Winnepesaukee has brought his wife or his mother or his girl to the big town. And aren't most New Yorkers from Winnepesaukee?'

'I suppose so,' I said. 'I'm an out-of-town youth myself.'

We talked about the hinterlands and the great open spaces and the lives of farmers and sharecroppers and small-town people. McCormack had a fine mind. He spoke in a school master's monotone, but his ideas were meaty. He had a direct approach to each idea he expressed. He talked slowly, wasting no words. He was talking with a purpose; he was building the conversation for a lead into the subject he really wanted to discuss. His manipulation of our dialogue fascinated me. We began with New York and soon arrived in Chicago, by way of a few idle remarks about big cities.

Big cities brought him easily to transportation. And transportation involved trains. From there on he romped home and it wasn't long before he recalled the train from Chicago and the terrible accident on the train and the man who had died.

'Scientists are stricken dumb, sometimes, when a casual death occurs under their noses. We face death daily in our laboratories and yet, when it strikes close to us we are continually amazed by it. Take that chap in the train. I've been thinking about him. I've been wondering about the procedure in a case like his.'

He was without guile. He looked up from his coffee and waited for my promotion of his idea.

I said: 'It's simple. The detectives came aboard in New York. They examined the body. They also examined everybody who had any contact with the body while he was moving on the train. After that, they took the corpse and went about their business.'

'So? The morgue was next, I suppose?'

'That's right. The autopsy.'

'And does it take a long time for them to reach a conclusion?'

'Not too long. They're pretty thorough down there. The mysteries of death are very few after the medical examiner gets through with the dead man.'

He thought that over for a while. 'And have they discovered the answer to the riddle?'

'What makes you think it's a riddle?'

McCormack shrugged and smiled a thin smile. 'He was a young man. I assume that there was an element of mystery involved in his sudden death.'

'You may be right.'

I allowed him a pause. In the silence he only stirred his coffee and continued his philosophical scrutiny of the spoon. The waiter brought him a piece of pie and he plucked at it with his fork.

'Do the police ever announce the result of the autopsy?'

'When they're ready to spill, they let the public know.'

'Very interesting. I understand his wife was with him on the train. It must have been a terrible blow to the poor woman.'

'So it was.'

'You know her?' he asked his pie.

'She's a client of mine.'

'How very interesting. You're not a detective?'

139

'Didn't you know?'

He put down his fork and stared at me. 'But, no. How could I have known you are a detective?'

'I don't keep it a secret.'

He wasn't offended. He continued to eat his pie until he had finished it. He gulped the dregs of his coffee and lit a cigarette. He took two drags, looked at his wrist watch, picked up both checks, and rose to leave. He shook my hand energetically.

'It's been nice seeing you. I'm at the International Hotel. If you're ever in the neighborhood, do drop by and we'll talk some more. I've always been interested in methods of detection.'

'Thanks. I'll do that. First chance I get.'

I watched him go. He left me as quickly as he had come. He was a spry and bouncing figure on his way to the door. At the door he turned suddenly and flipped me a good-bye with his hand.

I finished my ninth cup of coffee and phoned Sybil. She was wide awake, her voice husky and full of undertones.

I said, 'Is your girl friend still with you?'

'A big deal,' said Sybil. 'He calls me up to ask me about my girl friend. What am I, a governess?'

'Anything but that, baby. Is Dolly still there?'

'I told you she'd leave, didn't I? She left.'

'How long ago?'

Sybil's voice toughened, in a nice sort of way. 'Hold on a minute, she punched the time-clock on the way out, but the ticket's in the outer office.' And then, 'Listen, Detective, what do I do with the eight-course dinner I made for you?'

'I can't use it now,' I said. 'But keep it warm for me.'

'I've been keeping it warm. It'll spoil. Where in hell are you, and why should I be interested?'

'I'm sitting up with a sick friend.'

'You mean Maxie is sick?'

'Not Maxie — me.' I waited for the laugh, but it didn't come. 'Look, Sybil, your old pal Dolly handed me a package of trouble today. I'm beginning to worry about her — in a professional way, of course. When did she leave your place?'

There was a short and petulant silence. 'What gives? Dolly left here about half an hour ago. I wouldn't worry about her if I were you. She's all right. Strictly all right.'

'No more tears?'

Sybil laughed at that one. 'Tears, did you say? You're killing me, Detective. What you don't know about women customers would fill a couple of libraries. Dolly and I went out to dinner — over at the Waldorf. She drank herself a fine dinner — about ten Manhattans and a chaser of Bourbon. Then we floated back here and she bent my ear with fairy stories for a while. She was as high as the hem on Gypsy Rose Lee's pants. I had to force her to go home, she was that happy.'

I looked at my watch. It was two fifteen. I said, 'That's all I wanted to know, sugar. Keep that stuff hot for me. I may be up some time soon.'

'Let me know when you want it,' she laughed. 'I'll put the heat under it for you.'

13

Mrs. Dolly DePereyra's sitting room was a symphony of Victorian furniture, a startling room that reeked of tradition and high polish and the skillful touch of the decorator's hand. Scattered throughout the place were many mahogany-framed chairs, lightly laced on the arms and backs, placed in just-so positions to blend with the dubious decor of the walls. The carpet was wine colored and as deep and cozy as a fur neckerchief. On the carpet, slightly off center, a curious horseshoe sofa squatted in sentimental splendor.

On the carpet, too, was Mrs. Dolly DePereyra. She lay on her back, arms raised over her long and flowing hair, as though she had been placed in that position by a flossy photographer of the Cecil Beaton school, or an uptown rapist of the catch-as-catch-can variety.

I had seen all this through the open hall

door. I closed the door behind me and entered to see more. I shook her gently and stood back waiting for her to respond. If she was drunk, she was potted. Nothing stirred but the small bow on her neckline, and the bow stirred slowly and evenly, in time with her breathing. She was asleep and dreaming. I lifted her and carried her over to the horseshoe sofa. I put a pillow under her head and stood back to examine her.

I found the kitchen and got a glass of water. A wet handkerchief on her brow made her eyelids flutter and after a while she opened her eyes. She closed them quickly and I had to move fast to stifle the scream that she aimed my way. I held my hand over her mouth and sat down alongside her.

I said, 'Relax, Dolly. I came up here to talk business.'

The sound of my voice unloosened her frightened frame. Her shoulders sagged back beyond normal and when she opened her eyes all the fear was gone.

She said, 'You frightened me. I was afraid he had come back.'

'He?'

She began to sob, quietly, and I let her enjoy herself.

I said, 'Try to relax and tell me what happened.'

'I don't know what happened,' she said. 'I walked in here alone after I had a couple of drinks with Sybil. It took me a long time to make it. I was afraid. I didn't like the idea of staying in our — in this apartment alone any more. So I stood out there in the hall for a while, bracing myself. Then I came in and lit the lights in the living room. I started to cross the living room when I heard a noise in my bedroom. I tried to scream, but I guess I didn't make it. There was somebody in my bedroom. I stood here petrified, listening for noises. When I heard him drop something in there I must have fainted.'

I said, 'You've been out cold, then, ever since you got back?'

She nodded. She rubbed her hand over her forehead and got up, slowly. A bowlegged cupboard stood at the far end of the room. She waved her hand at it sleepily. 'I need a drink.'

I got a bottle and filled two glasses. She accepted the glass with a shaking hand, but managed to down half of the liquor in it without trembling at all. When she sat again I put my glass down and went into the bedroom.

It was a masterpiece of upheaval. A small desk in the corner of the room had spewed its contents on the rug. There was a galaxy of assorted stationery, small papers, large papers and the accumulated odds and ends of housekeeping ledger work. Two chests had been completely and systematically rifled. Assorted masculine and feminine apparel hung from every open drawer. Two small night tables had been pulled out of position and one of them leaned on its side against the big double bed.

The bed was as neat as the morning after a honeymoon. The sheets and blankets were piled in a helter-skelter mound at the footboard. The mattress itself had been pushed out of position and hung over the side. Somebody had

146

suspected the bed and knocked himself out trying to prove a point.

I returned to Dolly, now at ease on the sofa. The drink was gone, but she still held the glass. I said, 'Let's start from scratch. You walked in, stood in the center of this room until you heard the noise inside. Then you fainted?'

She nodded at the glass.

'You heard the noise, but saw nobody?'

'I couldn't have moved if I had wanted to. I fainted.'

'How did you know it was a man?'

She looked at me and made an attempt to smile, but it didn't quite come off. 'I didn't know, of course.'

'You assumed it was a man?'

'Are there many women burglars?'

'There may be a few floating around the city. Think back. What did you actually hear just before you fainted?'

She made an effort to think back. 'The noise. Something had been dropped. It was a loud thump, loud enough to frighten me to death.'

'A drawer, probably, hitting the rug. And that's all you heard?'

'That's all I can remember.'

'You heard no talking?'

She eyed me with befuddlement. 'Talking? You think there might have been two of them?'

'I don't know. I'm only trying. Somebody had a hell of a good time in your bedroom. Whoever it was, he knew that what he wanted from you couldn't be found in any other room in the house. Isn't that rather interesting?'

If it was interesting, she didn't let me know about it. She looked up at me dumbly and said nothing.

I said, 'Why should a common crook come into an apartment of this type and head straight for the bedroom? Why not the living room? You've got a lot of booty in this room — and there must be plenty in your silver chest in the dining room. A sensible apartment house plunderer would have rifled the place for the sort of junk he could peddle without too much trouble — silverware, for instance. Yet our man stayed in the bedroom and never came out of there. Why?'

148

'I don't know,' Dolly said, numbly. 'I can't imagine.'

I said, 'Suppose you come inside with me and take a look around?'

Dolly got up and followed me into the bedroom. She paused on the threshold and put a white hand to her throat to register surprise and shock and incredulity. She shook her head sadly and her wide-open eyes flitted over the panorama of disarray. She took a few tentative steps and then stopped at the bed. She sat down hard and said, 'I don't understand all this. I just don't understand it.'

'Let's try. See if you can discover what's been taken.'

She crossed the room and began to examine the chests.

'Jewelry,' I said. 'Look for your jewelry first.'

'There's no jewelry in the place worth anything at all. Before we left for Chicago I took all my jewelry down to the safe-deposit box and left it there.' She was bent over a small box, a jewel box. She had taken it from the top drawer of the chest. She held up a string of small pearls, finally. 'You see, even this wasn't touched. Of course, it's only a cheap one. And here's a gold ring I had left behind, too.'

'Never mind the cheap stuff. Wasn't there anything else he might have taken?'

'How could there be? It's all down at the bank.'

I took a walk for myself. I chewed a knuckle and did a few turns of the rug. The windows on either side of the bed were locked. I stared at them for a while, but they told me nothing I didn't already know.

I said, 'Whoever came in, used the hall door, and left that way. That's upper-crust burgling. That's robbery of the higher and more refined type. There's been an epidemic of this kind of thing in New York lately. The clever marauder enters by the front door — with a key. He knows his customers. He walks in, makes himself at home, takes what he wants and then leaves like a gentleman. No fuss. No bother. And enough booty for the wife and kids.'

She just sat there with her eyes closed,

tonguing her lower lip. She wasn't listening to me. So I kept right on, talking to myself.

'I can follow him up in the elevator, into the hall, at the door, inside this apartment — and then he leaves me cold. And worried. Why did he break in? If not for jewelry, why?'

Nobody answered, so I repeated my dialogue. 'If he didn't break in for jewelry, what else did he want?'

Dolly stood up and walked out of the room. I followed her. She led me into the little bowlegged cabinet and poured each of us a drink.

'I can't imagine,' she said. 'I wish I could help you. I wish I could tell you what he wanted — but I don't know.'

'Your husband,' I said. 'Suppose he were after something belonging to your husband — '

She played with the idea for a moment. 'I wouldn't know about that.'

'Think a bit. Did your husband ever keep important papers in the bedroom?'

'Papers?'

'Papers, documents, letters, records,

business files, blueprints?'

She waved them all away with a sigh. 'I really didn't know anything about Michael's business.'

'Notebooks, drawings, jottings, dottings, diaries?'

'I don't know.'

'Photographs?'

'I don't know.'

We weren't getting anywhere. I said, 'I'm wandering around in a dark hall on this thing. I'm all alone. My eyes are blindfolded and I'm in a dark hall all alone and groping for a door. It's not a very cosy position. Somebody came up here a few hours ago and went through your bedroom looking for an important item. We must assume that it wasn't jewelry or silverware or your fancy underwear. He came in here hell bent on finding something out of your husband's past. Why?

'Your husband is dead — maybe murdered. He might have been put out of the way because he had an enemy — a somebody who hated him enough to want to bump him off. Yet — you know nothing — nothing at all about your husband's business or his friends or his enemies. You're not helping me. You're not handing me a thing to hang on to. Surely you can give me some little scrap. Think hard. Think back. Did your husband ever keep papers in the bedroom?'

She did her best to help me. She sat there and rubbed her brow and bit her lip and tried. But she found nothing.

I toured the rug again, watching her struggle for a memory. The little devil in the lump behind my ear began to pound away at my brain and the pounding irritated me almost as much as Dolly DePereyra.

I said, 'I know who the woman was.'

'The woman?' She whispered it at me.

'The last woman he had anything to do with.'

I watched her closely, but she followed through in character. She held the glass in both hands now, tightly. When she opened her mouth to speak it was with a great effort. 'Who was she?'

'Gertrude Brown.'

She shook her head again and said nothing.

'An attractive woman, this Gertrude Brown.'

'How interesting.'

'A woman with great strength of character.'

'Really?'

'But you don't know her, of course?'

'Of course not,' she said, making a great show of annoyance.

'Too bad. I wish you had known her.'

'I don't want to hear any more about her.' Dolly got up, suddenly. She walked away from me.

I followed her and put my hands on her shoulders and when my hands touched her she stiffened and then sagged a bit.

'Sure you want to hear about her,' I said. 'I've just seen her.'

I felt her stiffen again. 'You work fast.'

'I have to work fast in my business.' I kept my hands on her shoulders and she didn't move away. I was talking to her hair-do. 'She knew your husband well. She had his picture on her night table.'

154

She shrugged my hands off her shoulders and faced me. Sudden color lit her cheeks and did no harm to her eyes.

'Keep it for your notes!' she said. 'I don't like to hear about Michael's women!'

She moved away from me again and sat. I followed her. 'We can't avoid talking about her, so why not be sensible about it? She was the most recent of his amours, therefore the closest to him recently. She's a fruity wench, this Gertrude Brown, given to muscular horseplay and fat friends. If I knew something more about her it would help me no end.'

'I don't know anything about her. How on earth did you find her?'

'At the station. I saw her down there this morning. She was waiting at the gate. She was waiting a long time.'

'For Michael?'

'Of course.'

'How do you know that?'

'I watched her. She hung around down there for a long time, waiting for somebody. When she saw you, she put on a big show of unconcern. She damn near

dropped her girdle, she was that uncon-
cerned. She knew you.'

Dolly got up again and walked to the
window. She stood there, looking out at
nothing but the night. She examined the
blackness for a while and then turned to
face me angrily.

'How could she know me?'

'I was going to ask you that question.'

'Don't bother. If she was down at the
station, I wouldn't have known about it. I
don't know her. I never knew any of his
women.'

'Of course not. Why does she excite
you so?'

'She doesn't bother me. How could she
bother me? But I loved my husband. If he
was murdered I want you to find his
murderer for me. I want to know why he
was killed. I want to see his murderer
burn. But I'm just damn fool enough to
still resent his girl friends. Is that funny?'

'I'm not laughing.'

'Thank you. All of this talk of women
brings back a bad part of the past. It
reminds me of how unhappy I was, do
you understand?'

156

She came back to me and sat down. There was something about the way she sat that bothered me. There was a feeling of closeness between us. It was a big sofa, but Dolly had chosen my end. She leaned on one hand and the hand was near mine. The smell of her perfume was strong. She breathed in an off-beat. Her breasts did things to the dress she wore.

I picked up my hat.

'Sure. Sure I understand.' I stood there, looking into her eyes and trying to understand her. She had lost all of her pallor. Her eyes were bright. There was a spot of color on her cheeks. She was suddenly a beautiful woman again, a new character, sensitive and highly desirable and very much alive.

I said, 'Whoever came here tonight won't return. You've got nothing to worry about. I'll see you again — soon. Just as soon as I have something to report.'

She came with me to the door and gave me her hand. 'You've been awfully kind, Steve,' she said. 'You're knocking yourself out for me and I want you to know how much I appreciate it.'

She didn't let go of my hand and we stood there for a moment looking at each other. Her eyes were as soft as her hand. Her eyes and her hand held me there for the split second interval that might have meant something more than appreciation.

When the elevator came she was still standing in the doorway, a pretty picture — a fleshy silhouette; sharp and clear and inviting.

14

It was mid-afternoon and we were sitting at the small table near the bay window again, Max and I.

The table was covered with Mrs. Dunwoodie's most festive linen. The afternoon sun highlighted her most elegant silverware and did the same to her chrome tresses. She flitted around us, brimming over with kind words and good intentions.

Max waited until she left the room. Then he swallowed the last dregs of his coffee in a noisy, purposeful gulp, pushed the cup away from him, lit a cigarette, blew smoke through his nose, blinked once or twice — and began to talk.

'The fat boy was plenty wise, Steve. He may be fat in the seat, but he has a good head — smart and sure of himself. He came out, just like you said he would, on the arm of a plainclothes dick. The dick was one of the crew we met down at the train the other day — the dirty-looking one they called Ferber. He and Ferber stood around for a while, just talking things over, like a bunch of college boys at a dance. Fat boy either knew Ferber, or he knows how to make friends and influence people quick. They stood around for maybe fifteen minutes that way. I could see by the way the fat John kept shifting his frame that he was plenty wise. He was standing there with Ferber for a reason — he wanted to make sure that nobody was on his tail. He kept turning on his feet, slow and easy like. He kept shooting his eyes this way and that, trying for a gander at anybody who might be hanging on his tail.'

'But he didn't see you?'

Max shook his head and smiled his sour smile. 'He didn't see me. He couldn't have. I was holed up in the fancy dump across the street. I knew this place would be safe — the boys in the hall were on my side because I had met them yesterday. Fat John couldn't see me because the lobby was darker than the inside of my pocket and he was looking from light to dark. After a while Ferber drove away in the squad car with his boys and the fat John started walking.'

'No cabs?'

'There were plenty of cabs. He didn't seem to want a cab. He started uptown, slow and easy, like a walk through the park. I figured he was playing it smart and simple — giving me a chance to come out of the hall and get after him. I figured that he wanted a good look at me and that was why he didn't take a cab.'

'I don't follow that part,' I said. 'He knew all about you, Max. Gertrude Brown must have described you right down the seams of your underwear. He didn't walk because he suspected you were following him.'

'That could be,' said Max, scowling in deep thought. 'Now that you mention it, you may be right. I'll tell you why. The fat John kept walking until he hit 82nd Street. Then he turned to the right and started across town. When he hit Lexington Avenue a funny thing happened. It was a little thing, but it may fit somewhere. When he hit Lexington Avenue he was going pretty slow — but I guess it wasn't slow enough for him. He stopped at the corner and leaned against a store window. He stood there, mopping his head, like a drunk with the blind staggers. He took off his little derby and just mopped his head and studied the sidewalk.'

'He couldn't have been drunk,' I said. 'When the cops walked in on him up in Gertrude Brown's apartment, he was either out cold or just coming to. We must assume that he was out cold — I hit him pretty hard. If Ferber found him that way he might have given him a small drink just to tone him up — but I can't picture dirty-vest Ferber allowing him to swill a bottle. And, besides, he wasn't weaving when he was talking to Ferber out on the street, was he?'

'Definitely not. He put on the first dizzy spell at Lexington Avenue and 82nd. This happened three times.'

'Three times? He kept right on walking?'

'He was strictly out for a walk. He went

down Lexington and he walked fine until he reached 67th Street. Then he leaned again, reached for his handkerchief again, and went through the same routine with the head mopping and slow roll of the head. The next time it happened was at Madison and 54th Street. It was very funny.'

'Funny?' I lit another cigarette and examined the tip of it for no reason at all. 'Maybe you were right about fat boy. He might have been trying for a gander at you by faking a weak spell. Did he turn his head and look for you while it was going on?'

'That's what I don't get, Steve. He didn't go phony on me at all. He looked like a very weak elephant leaning the way he did. If I hadn't been tailing him, I would have tried to help him.'

'How long did the spells last?'

'At least five minutes each.'

'He's sick,' I said. 'I hit him hard enough to knock some of his fat out of bounds. I probably loused him up, but good, when I hit his fat bay window with my shoulder. Come to think of it, he went down too quickly and gave up too easily. I probably dislocated his inner man.'

'You must have done something like that,' Max said. 'Because after the third spell, he gave up the idea of walking any more. He waddled into the street and hailed a cab and I followed him. He took me through the park once — all the way around.'

'That proves it, Max. He was out for the air. He was sick.'

'We got out of the Park on the 59th Street exit and from there he drove to an all-night cafeteria.'

'How long was he inside?'

'Not long at all. Ten minutes.'

'Coffee,' I said. 'He needed a bracer.'

Max said, 'You're talking this out like Dunninger. But you're probably right. He had the cabby wait while he went inside. When he came out he was walking much steadier, much faster. From there he drove to his hotel.'

'Which hotel?'

'The International.'

Max pulled out a small piece of paper. 'Hiram Goodson,' he read. 'Room 1509.

Registered over a year ago. A steady. Lives alone. Business — they know from nothing about his business at the desk. Habits? He has dough, spends it free and easy and is a good tipper. Regular hours. Gone most of the day. Leaves in the middle of the morning and comes back to eat dinner at the hotel as regular as clockwork. When he goes out at night he's sometimes late, sometimes early. Keeps to himself, but not unfriendly. That's what they gave me at the desk.'

'Visitors?'

'No visitors.'

'Dames?'

'No dames. I got that from the boys on the elevators. He's a clean John, fat boy is — must keep his women outside the hotel.'

'And keeps them well, if Gertie Brown is a sample. What next?'

'Plenty next. Where do you think fat boy Goodson was the last week or so?'

'He's been away?'

'He's been traveling. He just got back.'

'Stop stalling, Max. Give it to me.'

Max chewed and swallowed a small

piece of toast. 'Chicago. He's been to Chicago.'

I sat down. 'How do you know?'

'The desk. They got him his tickets. He came back when we did, Steve.'

'I'll be damned! You think he might have been on our train?'

'Why not? It was a big train, with lots of people on it. He didn't have to work hard to lay low on an overnight trip, did he? He could have stayed in his room until we pulled in, couldn't he?'

'But we would have seen him at Grand Central. We couldn't have missed him.'

Max gurgled. 'We could have missed him like nothing at all. We didn't give him a chance to come out, maybe. Maybe he just got up late and left the train after you sent me tailing Gertie Brown. The point is he got back from Chicago when we did. That puts him where we want him for DePereyra. It also makes me think.'

I tapped his head. 'Don't bother, Max. You're thinking that maybe Gertie Brown was on the train, too?'

'That's right. She could have been.

166

They might have fixed to meet after the train got in.'

'Why would she wait in the station? Why wouldn't she get in touch with fat boy on the train?'

'You sure ask the dumbest questions. I wish I were smart enough to give you the answers.'

I said, 'We'll get the answers.'

'Maybe we ought to get clever and go down to the police dicks for advice. Heath may know something.'

'Heath knows less than we do. We've got a few openings. But we've got a few too many.'

I got up and began to walk and chew my knuckles and make faces at the wallpaper.

The phone rang. It was Harry Bender.

Harry said: 'That roll of film you gave me. What's the gag?'

'The gag? You tell me.'

'I wish I could. I put it through my dark room. All I got was plenty of nothing. Nothing at all.'

'No pictures?'

'Nothing. Somebody might have snapped

some pictures on that roll. But the film must have been exposed when transferring it from the camera to the box. All I get is a fog. I see a dirty fog and a lot of light streaks across the field.'

'Light streaks? Isn't that unusual?'

'It's so unusual that it's been keeping me up, Steve. Last night I pulled that film out of the hypo and I've been studying it ever since. Ordinarily, when a roll of film is ruined that way, the ruination is complete. Your roll, however, isn't quite that dead. It seems to me that somebody attempted to photograph a manuscript.'

'A manuscript? What kind?'

'I can't read it,' said Harry. 'I can only catch the traces of typewriting on a white sheet. It's very very dull, but I'd swear it was a shot of a manuscript!'

'What else?'

'The roll shows streaks. Light streaks. They seem to be in a definite pattern, above the manuscript's blurriness. You follow me?'

I said, 'Not quite. What kind of patterns do you mean?'

'You'll find them something like streaks

— as if somebody had tried to photograph a series of fluorescent lights in a dark room. Is that what you were trying to do?'

I laughed at him. 'I wasn't trying anything. They're not my films. The business of photographing a manuscript may fit. But I can't understand those light streaks. What would cause them?'

'You're the detective. You tell me.'

'I'll tell you later. Put those negatives in a safe place, Harry. I have a feeling I'm going to need them.'

I hung up and Max allowed me to stroll the carpet for a while. I did four circuits of the living room.

Max said, finally, 'Put it down, Steve. Drop your pratt for a while. You're knocking yourself out.'

I told him about the film and the light streaks. He sat there scowling at the table cloth. 'I got some dope on things like that up here.' He tapped his forehead. 'I got it filed away in what I call my file of useless information. It's something I read in a science magazine lately. It's something about X-rays.'

'It's what about X-rays?'

'You can kill film if you expose it to X-rays, I think. Is that a help?'

'Maybe. The way I feel about this deal, anything might be a help.'

'It could be easier, the deal. It could be easier if we knew how DePereyra was knocked off, for instance.' He was talking to himself, too.

'The morgue reports it a natural death.'

'It's possible. Some people die natural.'

'Not this one. This one smells, for my money. Heath may have found something special. He's just slob enough to play it cagey. I don't blame him. He'd release it as death from natural causes while his hounds smell around for angles.'

'That could be,' said Max. 'I admit Heath isn't the dope I figure him. But this one is different. I add it up that the jerk died from natural causes.'

'Oh, sure. Michael DePereyra died from a bad gut ache, Max. It all adds up. It fits like the uniform they gave me when I joined the army.'

'How about his wife? She didn't think he died from natural causes, did she?'

'She didn't say.'

'She said plenty. Why should she get hot pants about spending good dough for a private eye if she thought he conked out natural?'

'Don't be funny. You forget that I found a bottle of rigor mortis in her valise, Max.'

'I don't forget anything. Are you figuring she gave you the business because she thought you'd blackmail her?'

'Why not? Mr. Heath would run her ragged if he knew about that bottle.'

'That could be,' Max said. 'But she ought to do us some good, Steve. She ought to have something for us.'

'She tries hard in her own cute way. She knows as much about her heel husband as we do. They had an ideal arrangement. She let him go out when his stud season hit him. He galloped off with the nearest blonde, and when he returned, there was his Dolly, all dressed up in a pink silk nightie, standing in the doorway and welcoming her hero home.'

'A couple of real home folks.'

'She's as steady as a skirt in a breeze. She's as fruity as a sailor's dream.'

Max showed me his knowing smile. 'You found out?'

'I didn't have time. But you don't need working time for a doll like Dolly. You can find her in the textbooks. The long-haired psychology boys would call her a 'charming psychopath'. You ever met one?'

'When I meet dames I don't bother with textbooks.'

15

That night I visited Louis Jennick.

Louis Jennick sat in a small, ill-lit room which, except for an old-fashioned desk, an old-fashioned lamp and a desk pad, might have passed for a closet in Gertrude Brown's emporium. There were two chairs; each ancient, each broken in the legs and back. There was a small clock on the wall, ticking its gears out in an overloud effort to keep the time. The carpet was as thick as sliced ham in a delicatessen sandwich. Through the door floated the smell of recently cooked cabbage.

There was a filing cabinet against the far wall, overflowing with papers and the assorted confusion of neglect. A small window faced a brick wall. Louis Jennick's midget frame squatted behind the desk. He picked at his front teeth, peered at me for a long pause, then threw away the toothpick and got up to shake my hand.

'A pleasure, Steve. What in hell you doing here, anyhow? You come down for some corned beef and cabbage?'

I said, 'I didn't come down here to eat, Louis.'

'It can wait. You still worrying about that stiff?'

'I'm not worried. I'm curious.'

His wife waddled through the door and stood there rubbing her hands on a dirty apron. She eyed me smilingly. 'Eat?'

Louis waved her away. 'Not now, Bella. Not now.'

I gave him a cigarette, dropped the pack on his desk and put myself down on one of his chairs carefully.

'Tell me all about it, Louis. What happened when the boys looked at him?'

Jennick shrugged. 'Nothing I could tell you about. Nothing at all. It was from natural causes, like I told you.'

'Says who?'

'Medical examiner says it. Also his assistant.'

'A routine check?'

'What do you mean, routine?'

'You know what I mean. Nothing funny?'

Louis took his feet off the desk with a sigh. 'It's official — strictly the last word. There were two men. One of them was Masterson, the medical examiner. Is this enough for you?'

'Maybe yes, maybe no.' I tossed my cigarette at the cracked enamel cuspidor and made it. I lit another cigarette and looked worried. Louis played with a mechanical pencil. He tapped the point on a piece of yellow paper. He punched out a design of tiny holes. He finished punching and crumpled the paper in his fist and threw it at the cuspidor.

I said, 'Suppose I'm not happy about it, Louis? Suppose I want to get something else?'

'Something else? Like what?'

'The stiff. What did they find on him?'

Louis threw up his hands and gave me a big show of frustration. 'I already told you it was natural causes. You don't believe me?'

'Sure I believe you. I'm forgetting

about all that. I want to know what they found on him.'

'On him? How should I know? They don't take that stuff down to the morgue, Steve.'

'You know Ferber.'

'Sure I know Ferber. So what if I know Ferber?'

'You know all the dicks, Louis. There were two other hard heads on the case with Ferber.'

'That's right,' said Louis. 'Man named Clark and man named Brunweiser. That's right.'

His wife came into the room, carrying a dish of fruit. She put it on the desk near Jennick's feet. He didn't move his feet away. He said, 'Not now, Bella. Thank you very much. But not now.'

She lifted the bowl of fruit and left the room.

I said, 'What has Heath got, Louis? What's the angle?'

He removed his feet from the desk with a great effort and belched loudly. 'I don't know what you're talking about, Steve. If I knew something special, who would I tell? Wouldn't I tell you, Steve? I ask you that.'

'Maybe if you told me, you'd go out of there on your ear. Maybe the boys said to keep your mouth shut.' He wasn't looking at me. He was rolling the pencil in his dirty hands. 'This DePereyra stiff was much too healthy to die from natural causes. And he died funny. Because of the way he died, I figure Heath will play the thing smart. If he has something, he's not going to spread it around until he needs it spread around. Isn't that the way he always operates?'

Jennick concentrated on the pencil. 'This Heath is plenty smart, for a cop.'

'That's why I came down here, Louis. I've got a customer, a rich dame who's paying me heavy sugar to do a job for her. I could get you a piece of change — '

He looked up at me and through me. 'She is paying you money because she thinks her man was murdered?'

'That's the idea.'

'And you think you can find him — the murderer?'

'I can try.'

'But you cannot try unless you know this DePereyra is murdered?'

I leaned both elbows on the desk. 'It might be a good idea for me to know that he was murdered. You know, Louis?'

He made a face full of lemon juice. He fiddled with his mustache and spat at the cuspidor. 'Ah — Christ! What do I say now?'

I said, 'I could get you one hundred bucks, Louis.'

He spat again. He came out from behind the desk and stood there with his hands shoved deep in his pants, staring at the carpet. He stood that way for some time, struggling with his small conscience.

'He was murdered?' I asked.

'All right! All right! He was murdered! Now you have enough? Now you can maybe leave me alone?'

I got up and slapped him on the shoulder. 'You're a pal, Louis, you're a real pal. Now I've got something to shoot for.'

He said, 'You got to keep it quiet. I didn't tell you a thing.'

'Sit down, Louis,' I said. 'Sit down and don't worry about it. You've just made yourself a hundred rugs — and you're going to be richer than that in about five minutes.'

He sat down. I gave him another cigarette. He sat there for a while, dragging on it gloomily. 'No more questions, Steve. You got what you wanted. That's enough.'

'Is a hundred bucks enough?'

'A hundred bucks is a lot of money. Plenty.'

'I can get you more than a hundred.'

He tried to shake the idea out of his mind. He shook his head and grimaced and held up his hands.

I said: 'I can get you two hundred more. That would make three hundred altogether.'

He opened his eyes and blew a silent melody through his long front teeth.

'That's big money. Real money.'

'It's as good as in your bank account, Louis. Open up.'

'You won't go shooting your mouth off?'

'Who can I tell? I'm in business for myself.'

'I lose my job if you shoot off your mouth,' he said. 'What I know I'm not supposed to know. You're not supposed to know.'

'Heath's instructions?'

Jennick nodded 'It's big.'

'How did you get it?'

'Ferber.' He laughed quietly. 'He was drunk. He's a big fool, that Ferber. Maybe I'm a big fool too, Steve.'

'Don't be a sucker, Louis. What you tell me is on ice.'

He squirmed in his chair and kept his eyes away from me. 'The money, when do I get it?'

'Right away. I'll send Max Popper down with it.'

'I guess I might as well give it to you, Steve. You talk awful fast. You got me sold.' He adjusted himself neatly in his chair. 'This stiff DePereyra did not die from natural causes. He was murdered. The medical men give him a big going over. They stayed with him a long time, shaking their heads. The little one, the assistant, won't let the medical examiner go home. He's smart, this assistant. He keeps telling the medical examiner the whole thing smells. They had a big argument and the boss, the medical examiner, he leaves. The assistant stays around for a long time, late. After a couple of hours, he goes home, too. But he comes back, quick, and starts in all over again. I hang around and watch. A couple of hours later he leaves the place, all excited.'

'He told you what he found?'

'Not him. Ferber,' said Jennick. 'Ferber came down later. He had a load on when he walked in. We went into the small office and he pulled out a bottle and we started to drink. After a while Ferber began to shoot off his big mouth.'

'Was he alone?'

'Ferber always drinks alone. That smart he is. I don't blame him, the way he drinks the stuff. We finished the bottle and then he started to talk. He told me that the stiff had been murdered.'

'How?'

'Poison.'

I got off my perch. 'Poison? What kind of poison?'

'Ferber had fancy words for the poison. I don't remember any of them.'

'The hell with the words, Louis. Tell me what you remember.'

Jennick massaged his brow and hand-picked his vocabulary. 'He said it is something to do with a new poison. This new poison is something different. It leaves nothing in the body. It kills fast and leaves nothing for the autopsy. The assistant was smarter than the medical examiner. The assistant has got the idea it is something very, very new.'

'And Ferber didn't mention the name?'

'Please,' Louis begged. 'Don't ask me the names. Let me think a minute.'

I gave him more than a minute. He drummed away on the desk and played games with his mustache. Finally he thumped a fist on the desk and said. 'It was something about radio.'

'Radio? You're nuts!'

'I can only tell you what I remember, Steve.'

'Radio?' I tossed the word around. I

threw it into my brain and let it simmer for a while. I got up and walked around, chewing my knuckle and murmuring the word. Then it hit me. 'Radium!' I said. 'Was it radium?'

'Radio.'

'Radioactive?'

'Ah! That's it. I remember Ferber saying it like that.'

'Radioactive poison?'

'You got it.'

I said, 'That's all you can tell me?'

'Isn't it enough?'

I slapped Louis on the shoulder and got up and put my hat on. 'You'll get your dough as soon as I see my customer, Louis. I'm off to the rat races.'

He came to the door with me, held my sleeve nervously. 'If it ever gets out, Ferber will knock my head off.'

'I never talk to cops,' I said.

When I ran down the ancient stairway, Louis was standing at the railing, looking down at me and shaking his head.

16

I spent the next afternoon at the International.

I knew two important members of the staff of the International. I had more than a nodding acquaintance with Lund, the house dick, a man of great integrity and unquestioned loyalty and boundless honesty and very few brains.

On my way to the desk, I circled the lobby away from a certain door and a certain small corner where I knew Lund would be.

My friend at the desk was Caldecott Chambers. Many years ago I had done a favor for Chambers and he was the sort of white collar mole who never would forget my face or the debt of gratitude he owed me. He was the assistant manager, a thin, small, sallow gentleman with a deep and penetrating memory.

His memory placed me in my proper niche and his hand was out for mine before I reached the desk. He took me inside and sat me down near him and gave me a small cigar and a wide smile and all the time I wanted.

I told him nothing but asked him plenty. His answers came slowly, only after he had checked them against the background of his memory. He went over the Goodson record and corroborated all of Max's information. He added nothing about Goodson's outside life.

I said: 'Is your list of steadies large?'

'Quite. This is a new hotel and we've always had people who want to live here permanently. We have an average middle-class rental on most of our rooms, and when the customers stay for a long time we make allowances to keep them here permanently. Good business.'

'And, Goodson — do you know where he came from?'

'I couldn't answer that. It's not our business.'

'Is it ever?'

He thought a moment. 'Sometimes, when we take on a phony who pays for a month and then decides to ride on his credit and skip. But Goodson is as regular as clockwork.'

'I don't blame him. It's a good hotel. It must be good to rate the convention of atomic brains you've got here. How'd you happen to get them?'

He smiled. 'One customer invites another. Miss Mary Wyndham brought that gang here, I'm sure.'

'How come?'

'She's a steady. She's had a room for the past six months.' He winked at me slyly. 'She doesn't do our place any harm, Steve. Best looking blonde I've seen in our lobby.'

'Or any other lobby,' I added. 'I know her.'

'A nice girl. And we'll never stop thanking her for bringing her uncle's group here. The publicity's been wonderful.'

I finished my cigar and thanked him and went out. I strolled the lobby of the International, playing games with myself and enjoying the ebb and flow of life before me.

The soft seats in the center were filled

with all manner of people: fat buyers from out of town, heavy-bottomed matrons on the loose for a fling in town, thin-legged girls gabbling in groups, and the flotsam and jetsam of characters from Broadway and Flatbush and the hinterlands of the big city.

It was a lush lobby, high ceilinged and bright with the gilt of classic decor. I circled it three times, measuring the crowd and keeping within eye-shot of the elevators. I leaned against the marble pillar and lit a cigarette and saw what I saw.

A man in a black felt hat slid through a door on the other side of the lobby, put a cigar in his face, bit it, lit it, puffed it, waved the smoke away from his eyes, adjusted his glasses and began to stroll through the crowd with his hands deep in his pants pockets.

The elevator on the left came down and emptied four people into the lobby. They were four men, each short, each fat, each smoking a cigar and gesturing.

The man in the black hat passed the phone booth, observed the lady in the green cloth coat, tipped his cigar ashes daintily and proceeded along the opposite wall past the small booth set up for The March of Dimes campaign.

A character in a gray topcoat leaned over a girl in a chair. The girl put down her magazine, stiffened, pulled her head back from him, laughed a hoarse laugh and said: 'Oh, Charlie, you frightened me!' Then Charlie slapped her knee, helped her stand and piloted her through the big door, over which a neon sign read: BAR.

The man in the black hat paused at the newsstand, handed a coin to the girl, got a cigar, buried the cigar in a vest pocket, smiled at the girl, chucked her under the chin and went away.

The right elevator came down, disgorged a group of middle-aged women. They were heavily made up, dressed fashionably, babbling at each other and outward bound.

The man in the black hat faced me from across the lobby. He was puffing his cigar madly. He made a great show of not noticing me. He tipped his ashes and started toward me through the crowd in the lobby.

A boy came into the crowd from the desk. He had a small silver tray in his hand. His uniform was tight, too tight for his buttocks. It made him walk with a short-stepped gait. He lifted his little face to the ceiling. He bellowed: 'Caaaaaaaaaal fooooooah Mistuh Greenwood — Mistuh Greeeeeenwood!'

The middle elevator came down, empty.

The bellhop with the tray passed close to me, still bawling: 'Caaaal fooooah Mistuh Greenwood — Mistuh Green-wood!'

I watched him disappear behind the row of phony palms near the cashier's window.

By the time I turned from watching a passing blonde, the man in the black hat was standing at my elbow. He kept his hands in his pockets and talked to me through the cigar.

'Who is it, Ericson?' he asked. 'Who you waiting for?'

I said, 'Hello, Lund. Where've you

been? I've been looking for you.'

'Sure. For the last half hour you've been breaking your neck trying to find me.' He removed the cigar and carefully dropped the ashes on my right foot. 'I wouldn't give a nickel for anything in the lobby you missed.'

'Thanks. I never would have guessed you were watching me, Lund.'

He breathed deep at that one, enjoying every word of it. 'I get around quiet like,' he said. 'In the hotel business you don't stand around. Who you waiting for?'

'Nobody.'

'You been standing there a long time waiting for her.'

I made myself laugh. 'You sure have a way of guessing things, Lund.'

He jerked the cigar out of his face and leaned toward me. He touched me on the shoulder with the hand that held the cigar and the five cent smell of it bit into my nostrils. He said, 'Deduction is all.'

'What a gift. You've certainly mastered the art of deduction, Lund.'

The left elevator came down. There were seven people in it, three men and four women. The women were together; they moved in a tight knot toward the bar and disappeared. A man in a Chesterfield and derby walked toward us through the lobby, paused at the palms, hesitated and then retraced his steps in a detour to the exit. It was Oscar Wyndham.

Lund said, 'There's a funny bird for you. Did you catch him?'

'Looks like he might be the absent-minded professor,' I said.

Lund slapped my shoulder. 'Now you're thinking. You hit him on the nose. He's a professor, all right — that was Professor Wyndham, one of those scientist fruitcakes. Crazy as a bedbug.'

'I wouldn't have figured him that way. He looks all right to me. How do you make him a dope?'

Lund smiled for his own satisfaction, a big boy with a secret enjoyment. 'I never thought I'd have any trouble with any of them college professor types. But this guy Wyndham certainly changed my mind for me. The other night, it was. Pretty late, too. He damn near split his gut he was so excited. He came down to my office at about midnight. He had just come back from a meeting somewhere and was about to hit the hay when he missed something. He came running into my office as pale as a ghost. He was in his robe, he was so excited.'

I chuckled because he wanted me to. 'What was he excited about?'

'This'll kill you!' Lund roared into a high gale of laughter. 'It'll murder you. I quieted the guy down and he told me what was the trouble. He told me he was missing a box.'

'A box?'

'That's right. A lead box filled with some kind of chemical. He claimed it was stolen from his room. He kept yapping about how valuable it was and then I damn near died. I asked him to quiet down and explain. It took him a long time to get control of himself and then he spilled. This box he was raving about was made of lead and weighed up pretty heavy.'

'Heavy? How heavy?'

Lund added confusion to his flat face. 'Heavy is all he said. The whole thing sounded crazy to me.'

'And somebody stole a heavy lead box from his room?'

'Crazy, isn't it?' Lund said. 'But that's all he gave me and when I try to break him down, when I try to find out why anybody would walk into his room and lug this box out, he freezes up on me and gives me some crap about atomic energy and stuff like that.'

'Did he tell you what kind of chemical he had in the thing?'

Lund thought back and scowled at his memory. 'I think he mentioned it — but me, I can't remember anything scientific like chemicals. I told him to go to sleep and forget it. I tried to brush him off. He finally went up to his room, but he called me every half-hour until four in the morning to see if I had done anything. Naturally, there wasn't much I could do for the guy. I had to wait until the morning to really make a search.'

'You notified the police?'

'Do I look nuts? What could I tell them? I notified nobody but my assistant and the manager. It was all to the good.'

He paused to allow himself the pleasure of self-adoration. 'It was all cleared up the next day.'

'He found it?'

'You guessed it. He found it in his own room, the nut. He had put it in the closet, behind his suitcase and just plain forgot about it. He sure looked like a dope when he explained it to me.'

'Like I said — the absent-minded professor.'

'That's right, at that. You hit him on the nose.'

The right elevator came down. Two men and a woman. One of the men was fat. He walked alongside the woman as they left the elevator. She turned her head to say a word to him, but didn't stop walking. The fat man smiled. She was a medium-sized blonde in a brown tweed suit. She carried a red handbag. Her hat was brown felt, cut to dip across the right eye. She walked with eye-catching grace. I recognized the walk and the walk was Mary Wyndham's. The fat man was Goodson. He left her at the potted palms and walked toward the bar. When she passed the palms, a man rose from a seat hidden in the foliage. He followed her.

I said, 'Got to go, Lund.'

'I don't blame you. Hot blonde.'

'You're terrific, Lund. Terrific.'

'Deduction is all.'

When I reached the revolving door, the blonde stood outside. A man faced her, talking fast. It was getting him nowhere. She was giving him ice, plenty of ice and head shaking. And it didn't bother him.

The man was Lester Henshaw. I walked through the door and put my right hand on his shoulder.

I said, 'Still bothering pretty women, Henshaw?'

Henshaw scowled, tried to shake my hand away, couldn't. He managed a soapy grin. 'Hello, Steve.'

The blonde gave me her smile. 'It's the detective hero!'

I shook her hand. 'Where would you have me bury this man, Mary Wyndham?'

'I'm not fussy. Any sewer will do.'

'You don't welcome his attention?'

'I can live without it.'

I tightened my grip on Henshaw. He squirmed. 'Take it easy, Steve. I was only trying for a story.'

I said, 'We made a deal, maggot brain.'

'I only wanted to ask a few questions.'

I shook him a bit, from side to side, until his coat didn't fit him. 'We made a deal.'

Mary Wyndham said, 'Don't hurt him, Steve. Just shake him once more and let him go. He'll find the sewer on his own.'

I shook him again. I shook him until his mouth hung open.

I said, 'Now crawl, Henshaw. You can't crawl far, but if you're smart you'll crawl to Grand Central and squirm into the first train out of town. The next time I see you, I won't play potsy.'

He slid out of my grip and ran down the street, a comic character on the loose.

Mary Wyndham watched him until he disappeared in the crowd. Then she turned to me and waited for my laughter. When I began to laugh she joined me in the hilarity. I took her arm and I said: 'He's pretty fast for a maggot. I've been hoping to see you. This is a lucky break for me.'

She looked down at my hand on her arm. She moved her arm up and down gently. 'And where do I find the strong man to pry me loose from you?'

I said, 'You won't mind me. I'll grow on you.'

'I was afraid of that.'

'I'm the good, clean detective type. I can do you no harm.'

'And how much good?'

'I tell funny jokes and do imitations. You don't have to listen. You can be eating.'

We had made Madison Avenue and her arm was still my property.

She said, 'Is all that good for a young girl?'

'Be a little more unselfish. Think of me. I could eat crow on a meat hook and enjoy it if you were there looking at me.'

'And if I refuse?'

'I'll crawl into the same sewer with Lester Henshaw.'

'That would be sad,' she said and

squeezed my arm. 'Where do you eat your crow, Steve?'

I called a cab and took her to Louis and Armand's.

17

Victor gave me my favorite corner, near the bar, hovered over us and made me feel important.

'Ah, Mr. Ericson,' he said. 'It is good to see you again. Where have you been keeping yourself?'

'I've been around, Victor. I've been making a fortune tracking down lost husbands.'

'Women pay for that?'

'Some women like their husbands. I've just met a woman who was crazy about her husband. Even cried when he died.'

We had a fine meal of guinea hen and wild rice. Mary Wyndham let me talk. I gave her a condensed history of the life and times of Steve Ericson. I gave her my likes, my dislikes and a running commentary on an assortment of topics. She had a good mind. She was quick and bright and enthusiastic when I wanted her to be. She listened well, stirred her coffee and gave me the brightness of her eyes and her smile and her easy laughter.

When I paused, finally, to light a cigarette, she said: 'That woman who cried when her husband died — was that the woman on the train?'

'Mrs. Dolly DePereyra — a character.'

'A character?'

'A character straight from a guidebook on psychiatry.'

'Most women have mental quirks. But so do most men. Why do you label her queer in the head?'

'I know her well. She's a customer of mine.'

Mary Wyndham was puzzled. 'Is she an old customer or do you go around picking up customers on trains?'

'I'm not fussy. I take my customers where I find them. Her husband died on the train. Can I help it if he chose my train to die on? He didn't die a clean death. She wants me to investigate. I investigate.'

She laughed at me. 'Don't tell me it's as easy as that to get paying customers. You're incredible.'

'It's not easy. You play along sometimes and get snarled up in a chain of lucky circumstances. You get on a train in Chicago. You meet a few people, have a few drinks. One of the people you meet is a woman. She sees another woman, an old friend, and introduces her to you. Then, a man dies. You step in and offer your services. Sometimes it works. Other times you are brushed off. It's simple when it's simple, it's tough and hopeless when it's tough and hopeless. Do I make sense?'

She didn't answer immediately. She sat there toying with her spoon, turning it in her cup and watching the swirl of the coffee. When she looked at me her eyes were full of an inner amusement.

'And how is your investigation coming?'

'I have two or three small threads. But the rug is a big one.'

'You're busy hunting down leads?'

'I'm busy doing nothing. I'm having a fine time chewing my knuckles.'

'You talk a good detour, Steve.'

I said, 'You're too smart to be a blonde.

You're too direct.'

She put down her spoon and leveled her eyes at me. 'I feel like a lost clue, just sitting around waiting to be discovered. Is that why you waited for me to ask me out to dinner?'

'Not exactly. I like you. I like to talk to you. Back on the train I knocked myself out waiting for you to come back to the club car. You never did. Why?'

'A girl my age needs her sleep.'

I said, 'You can help me.'

'Of course. You want to ask me a few questions? About the train?'

I reached for her hand. She didn't pull it away from me. She allowed me to pat it and squeeze it.

'You won't be angry with me?' I asked.

'Don't give me the chance, Steve. What do you want to know?'

I began with DePereyra. 'All things have a beginning, Mary. When did you meet Michael DePereyra?'

'When? The evening the train pulled out of Chicago.'

'You didn't know him before then?'

She shook her head. 'He's not my type.'

'Yet you got to know him on the train. Why?'

She gave the water glass her smile. It was a thin smile, aimed into her own subconscious. 'How can I explain a thing like that? I was sitting in the club car reading a magazine and Michael DePereyra sat alongside me. He wanted to make conversation. I didn't see any reason for snubbing him. You know how it is on trains. Everybody more or less lets their hair down. He wasn't particularly objectionable so we had a conversation.'

'About what?'

Her eyes clouded over the question and I thought I saw a glint of anger deep inside them. 'Aren't you being a bit too personal?'

'Shouldn't I be? If you had just met him, why not tell me what was cooking? It may help me. He had a very jealous wife.'

Mary Wyndham shrugged delicately. 'I suppose you're right. I should tell you. He was putting on an act for me, I suppose. He was playing the scene heavy, overacting. He was trying to get me to believe that he was stricken with me.'

'And that's all?'

'You expected more?'

'I apologize. I'm trying to set Michael into the scene. How many times did you see him in the club car?'

'Twice. The first time we were alone. The second time he came in while I was reading a magazine. That was when I met you.'

'And after that?'

'I didn't see him after he left the club car.'

'Did you know he was married when you met him the first time?'

She laughed. 'How could I? Did you expect him to tell me about his wife and make a play for me at the same time? That sort of technique never works, does it?'

'I've heard differently. But we'll skip it. Did he tell you anything about himself?'

'He was too busy talking about me.'

'An eager beaver, eh?'

'An eager wolf.'

'You gave him no time?'

'Are you trying to be funny?'

'I'm trying to be serious,' I said. 'This

isn't a funny case at all. If DePereyra was encouraged it might be important. After all, he did come back to talk to you, didn't he?'

'That type always does.'

'Even without encouragement?'

Mary Wyndham colored. The flush affected her eyes. They shone with a deeper glow now. They shone with embarrassment, not anger.

She said, 'I don't know what you're getting at, Steve. I'm not used to talking to detectives. If you mean that I encouraged him the first time I met him and therefore he came back for more, you're dead wrong. I gave him no time at all when I met him. He wasn't the type to give up. He came back for another brushoff.'

'I apologize again. I'm straining for information on this thing. I've got a weird cast of characters, each one a lead, yet all of them of no use to me. DePereyra was a type of lunatic, I suppose.'

'A lunatic?'

'A borderline case, if not completely nuts. His wife would look well in a mental home, too. I've read about people like Dolly DePereyra in mental cases from the medical library. If he was queer, she's worse. But a city like New York is loaded with queer people. I suppose you've seen a lot of them at the hotel?'

She laughed. 'The International has a popular lobby. Sometimes I just sit around and watch the types that gather there.'

'Do you know anybody in the hotel?'

'Why should I?'

'You've had a room there for a long time.'

'You really are a detective!' Mary smiled and showed me her beautiful teeth. 'How on earth did you find that out?'

'I get around. You've had the room for six months or so?'

'Wonderful!'

I played with my spoon. 'What did you do with it? How could you keep it while you were in Chicago?'

She held a pretty hand to her mouth in mock secrecy. 'You won't tell?'

'Promise.'

'Subleased it,' she whispered. 'Rented it to a girl friend of mine just so's I could have it whenever I came into New York. Not bad for a blonde, eh?'

'I've always believed blondes were smart.' I reached for her hand and patted it. She didn't seem to mind. 'And who was that big fat man who came down with you in the elevator? I'm jealous.'

'Mr. Goodson?' she tittered. 'Poor old Goodson — he's been trying to get acquainted ever since I came in from Chicago. He's rather pathetic. You've got nothing to worry about.'

I said, 'I worry about the craziest things at the craziest times. You won't hold it against me?'

She smiled her answer and I reached across the table to get her hand. She let me have it. I ordered two Old Fashioneds and we downed them in fast conversation and much laughter. She was a good drinker, and the alcohol did nothing more to her than a slow unbuttoning of her libido. We had two more and left the place.

I took her to the Frigate, an intimate

little bar on the West side. We sat there for a long session of boogie-woogie. We sat together on the red leather wall seats designed for leg rubbing and the more polite over-the-table intimacies. A black pianist hammered out a fancy bass and showed his teeth to the smoke and bad air. We had three more Old Fashioneds and went out of there.

We walked arm in arm along the dark streets and arrived at Broadway. We took a cab and in the cab she was close to me, half asleep on my shoulder. I lifted her head and she laughed at me in the drowsy way a woman laughs when she means something more than laughter.

I said, 'Whither away, now, fair one?'

'Meaning what?' she asked. Her voice was low and strange and I didn't mind the strangeness.

I tapped the driver on the shoulder and he took us to the International. We managed the lobby without being seen by Lund. We entered the place from the east side, away from the lobby and the bar and the hurly-burly at the desk. She walked steadily, but clung to my arm and didn't release me until she had closed the door to her room and we were alone.

The room was of medium size, but it had a freshness and charm uncommon to the usual static hostelry set-up. There were traces of feminine decor added in the right spots. Well framed pictures lined the walls. Odd pieces of good furniture were scattered in odd places.

There was the small divan, for instance, on which Mary Wyndham had settled herself in a pleasant posture.

'All the comforts of home,' she said.

I joined her on the divan. The feeble glow from a small desk lamp promoted the shadows in her eyes. I lifted her chin and kissed her lightly and she seemed to like it, so I said, 'Home was never like this.'

She answered with her hands. She put her hands around the back of my neck and brought my head down and this time she kissed me. She kissed me soundly, putting her body and the full strength of her arms into it. It was a pleasurable kiss. I closed my eyes and decided to enjoy it.

She ran her fingers through my hair

and we talked of life and love and the detection of crime.

I said: 'Maybe you'd better forget I'm a detective now.'

'I'll try, Steve. You make it pretty easy.'

'Thanks.' I pulled her to me and kissed her again. 'It shouldn't be too tough. I'm doing as much good on this case as a certain city dick I know. I'm knocking myself out on the two or three threads I've told you about.'

'And you thought I was another thread?'

'You? Never.'

'Not even a small thread?'

'Not even a stitch. What I've got is strictly for a scientific mind.'

She sat up and eyed me quizzically. 'Did you say scientific?'

'Better than that. I should have said super-scientific.'

'I could serve you in that department. I've got connections to some of the best scientific craniums in the world.'

I kissed her again. 'I'm glad you suggested it. Can you get me a short chat with the famous Professor Frotti?'

She made a face at Frotti. 'I can, but I won't, He's not good enough for you, not smart enough.'

'You should know. Who would you suggest?'

She thought a moment and then laughed. 'Uncle Oscar, of course!'

'Can I get him now?'

Mary looked at her watch. 'It's eleven-thirty, but we can try.' She picked up the phone and spoke to her uncle. She told him about me and there was a short pause while she listened. When she put down the phone she was smiling again.

'You can go right up, Detective.'

18

Oscar Wyndham had a warm handshake, a warm greeting and a rich, warm voice. He was tall, a shade taller than I. He dressed in the manner of the dignified professionals, but he might have been a rich Wall Street man; an executive, a director of a corporation, a tycoon.

He had broad shoulders, and the cut of his gray double-breasted suit was carefully planned to promote them. His face was long, but not thin, and he had a fine nose and two of the blackest eyes in the world. His dark eyebrows and raven hair did much to exaggerate the dignity of his features. He had a musician's mane of hair, neatly combed in a pompadour that began high on his brow in a sharp widow's peak.

He mixed two glasses of Scotch, handed me one, motioned me into a seat and said: 'I remember seeing you in the train. In the club car.'

'You've got a good memory.'

'Oh, no,' he laughed. 'It's a trick — all memory is a trick. You can train yourself to remember all kinds of things, people, dates, facts and figures. A man with a good memory is outstanding only because he has taken the time to make his memory work for him. It is a matter of great importance in my business.'

He began a short dissertation on the scientific approach to the business of memory. I let him talk because I was enjoying the sound of his voice. It was almost hypnotic. He spoke softly, yet there was a ring and a power to everything he said. It was a voice to command respect and attention from students in a classroom. It was a voice that could work wonders with women. I wondered how much it had done for him in that direction.

He was sharp enough and wise enough to bring his lecture to a quick finish. He said, 'But you didn't come up to visit with me so that I might lecture. I suppose, since you are a detective, you've come about the incident on the train?'

'I want to ask you a few questions. Do you mind?'

'Ask away.'

I brought out one of my index cards and studied it. I gave him enough time to deduce that my question might be important because of the index card.

I said: 'Did you know Michael DePereyra?'

'No, I did not. I heard his name only after he died on the train.'

'Then you didn't meet him on the train?'

He shook his head. 'Obviously not.'

'How about the others?'

'The others?'

'The rest of the scientific boys, I mean. I'm referring to two of them especially. Frotti, for instance.'

'I've never heard Professor Frotti mention him.'

'And McCormack?'

'Nor McCormack.'

I said: 'That's too bad.' I studied the filing card for a while, sighed over it, tapped it with my index finger and put it away. I let the silence grow between us. I sipped my drink and made a great show of uncertainty and perplexity.

Wyndham sat there watching me.

'I don't suppose you know much about the case?' I asked.

'Only what I've read in the papers.'

'The papers have told the public nothing. I know a little more than the man in the street because I was assigned to the case by the wife of the dead man.'

'Assigned?'

'I got the job on a hunch. I figure Michael DePereyra was murdered.'

The black eyebrows lifted. 'Indeed?'

'Because I think that he was murdered I've been following through, Wyndham, gathering a bit here and there, but not enough for any great deductive conclusion. I came up here to see you because I thought you might help me.'

'I understand. You have a clue?'

'I have a theory. But my theory is strictly lay thinking. I've got to have somebody — a scientist like you — set me straight and strengthen or kill my theory.'

He spread his hands. He gave me a chuckle and leaned forward. 'But I'm not that type of scientist, Mr. Ericson. Remember, I've been more or less a specialist for a good many years.'

'Mary's told me. My questions are right up your alley.'

He settled back again. 'Then fire away.'

I fired.

I said: 'Tell me something about arsenic.'

'Arsenic? That's sort of a broad subject. What do you want to know about it?'

I assumed the classic schoolboy face, full of wonder and stupidity and a rapturous willingness to learn. 'Everything,' I said. 'You can start from the beginning with me. I'm stupid, but I'm willing to learn.'

Wyndham showed me his boyish smile. 'A doctor could tell you about its use as a tonic in medicine, a metallurgist could tell you how it's used in low-melting solders, a chemist might tell you its typical reactions, and a nuclear physicist can tell you how many isotopes it has, and what their properties are. What sort of 'something about arsenic' are you looking for?'

216

'I'll take as much as you can give me, in easy doses.'

'Perhaps you want the medical angle? In that case you're asking questions of the wrong kind of doctor — you need an M.D., not a Ph.D.'

'You sound like the right teacher for me. I didn't know arsenic was a tonic in medicine,' I said. 'I had an idea it was strictly a sleeping medicine — a good prescription for permanent shut-eye.'

Wyndham shook his head and grinned. 'I'm not a medical man, but I happen to know it's a first-rate blood-builder, appetite builder and nerve tonic. Yet, oddly enough, it takes about eighty times as much arsenic to kill a medium-sized dog as it takes to kill a large man, if it's taken as arsenic oxide.'

I pulled at my nose, straining to stay out of my depth in the deep water. 'Arsenic oxide? You're too far ahead of me, Wyndham. A moron like me must walk slowly and think at the same stupid pace. Just what is the low-down on arsenic?'

He began to explain. He talked slowly

and tapped two fingers on his palm to keep himself on the beat. 'Arsenic itself is a grayish, crystalline metal — incidentally very hard to handle in a cyclotron; it keeps giving off gas that gets in the way. But the 'arsenic' poison or tonic is a compound of the metallic element with oxygen, usually, or a nitrate like that. All of which is a very mildly poisonous form of arsenic. The really nasty one is *arsine* — a compound of arsenic and hydrogen.'

'A gas?'

He nodded. 'An extremely poisonous gas. So poisonous that it makes the ordinary arsenic oxide poisons — or even the famous cyanides — seem as harmless as table salt. One small bubble of the gas has been known to kill a man.'

I whistled. 'Is it easy to concoct?'

'It's very easy.' He got up and crossed the room for a package of cigarettes. 'Does all that interest you?'

'You're making me think,' I said. 'I always figured you atomic boys as fiddlers with cyclotrons and uranium-piles and all that sort of guff. You're opening a new corner of my feeble mind, Wyndham.'

He returned to his chair and lit his cigarette. 'A nuclear physicist is interested in the insides of atoms, and what makes them tick, or not tick. But he's got to handle atoms as they appear in Mother Nature. For instance, if you want to bombard oxygen with deuterons in a cyclotron, it gets just a bit tricky if you try to use oxygen itself. The stuff's a gas, and won't hold still while you take pot shots at it with twenty million volts. So you've got to tie it down somehow — use an oxide instead of oxygen. A nuclear physicist needs chemistry to make his nuclei stand still for him. Do you follow me?'

'I'm holding my own.'

'Good,' he said. 'Now, before you begin to dabble with chemicals, it's usually considered smart to have a damn good idea which ones are apt to crawl out and bite you. You think of uranium and plutonium as the atom-bomb stuff, but we have to consider the fact that uranium is a hard, brittle, very dense metal that is extremely tough to machine on a lathe, and corrodes rapidly in contact with water. Sure, it's the atom-bomb metal, but before it blows up, it has to be handled as a metal, just like any other metal.'

He waited for my nod and went on. 'But before it's a metal, it's an ore, and has to be separated by chemistry. It happens that uranium compounds are extremely poisonous, too. In the Manhattan Project, the safety precautions included guards against radioactive poisoning, precautions against dropping a very ordinary sledge hammer on the toe, and regulations to keep the deadly chemical poisons, uranium and plutonium oxides and hydroxides, out of the workers.'

He was making it awfully clear, so clear that my head throbbed with a sudden excitement. I said: 'Maybe I see what you mean, Wyndham. Since uranium is radioactive, if you eat some it's poisonous. Is that what you mean by radioactive poisoning?'

He shook his head patiently. 'Not at all. That would probably be poisoning by a radioactive, I suppose. The poisoning is chemical, do you understand?'

'Say it again.'

'I'll break it down,' he said. 'If an Indian shot a Pilgrim with an arrow, the feathers on the arrow just came along for the ride. They didn't kill the Pilgrim. Similarly, if you poison a man with a chemical, the fact that the chemical may or may not be radioactive makes no difference. He died of chemistry, not radioactivity. Radioactivity is something totally different. The radiations given off by radioactive materials, like radium, or the synthetic radioactive materials we can make either in a cyclotron or by exposure to the radiations of a functioning uranium pile — are the real, honest-to-God death rays. Gamma rays can kill in a dozen different ways, depending on how much you get. A light dose, continued for a long time, will cause cancers, or a radiation anemia. A massive dose for a shorter time will kill by destroying the source of the white blood cells, so that the body's defending army is killed off, and the next invading germ can cause death.'

I whistled again.

'It gets more horrible as we explore,' said Wyndham. 'A really massive blast of gamma rays can destroy human tissue in a matter of minutes or hours after exposure. All the cells of the flesh are killed; the man dies instantly if he is struck in a vital organ, in a matter of hours if the extremity of a limb is hit. Gamma rays are death days. People think that atomic bomb was something. But we can manufacture synthetic radioactives that will give off such floods of these gamma death rays that entire cities can be wiped out. All this is radioactive poisoning — radioactive rays turning the flesh of the body itself into poison that destroys man.'

A small, cold tremor eased itself away from the base of my brain and began to crawl, willy-nilly, down my spine. 'You make a man worry about his bomb-proof shelter, Wyndham.'

Wyndham laughed. 'Don't build it unless you can make it a ray-proof shelter, Ericson. There's nothing that can hide a man from an atomic bomb, unless you make your shelter ten feet thick in the walls and be sure to build the walls of barium sulfate plaster, or four feet of boron steel. That might stop the rays.'

'Ten feet thick, did you say?'

'Approximately. Gamma rays from radium can get through 20-inch thick steel. But radium is nothing to what we can manufacture now.'

He was giving me ideas, too quickly for complete cataloguing in my already crowded cranium. 'Then radioactive poisoning can be done from a distance? From one room to another? From one house to another?'

'Certainly,' he said. 'Some of the really hot radioactives can cause appreciable gamma ray activity at a distance of three quarters of a mile in the air. Ordinary walls don't slow them up.'

I fumbled with a fresh cigarette. In the pause, I backtracked to another angle. 'Could ordinary arsenic be made radioactive?'

'It would be only gilding the lily,' smiled Wyndham. 'There are four or five forms of radioactive arsenic, but making arsenic radioactive is rather futile. It happens that the radioactive arsenic isotopes are all low-energy isotopes, and give relatively low-power gamma rays. Arsenic, particularly in the form of arsine, is deadly enough without trying to make it radioactive. There'd be no — well, maybe there would, at that.' He put a hand to his eyes and began to massage the bridge of his nose.

'Suppose,' I said, 'a murderer made this arsine radioactive and used it to kill? He'd have a good chance to get away with it if — '

Wyndham held up a hand. He was smiling again, but this time there was a spark in his eye. 'You're stabbing, Ericson. You're making a good try for a scientific angle, and for all I know you may have something. A murderer could do a job with arsine, and having done the job would probably escape detection. It takes so little arsine to kill a man that only the most delicate chemical tests would reveal it at all. Ordinary tests are intended to prove that Joe Doakes poisoned Josie Doakes with arsenic. The body is usually loaded down with the poison. But if a man were poisoned with radioactive arsine, chemical detection would be awfully difficult, damn near impossible. The stuff would turn into the element called germanium in a short time. Germanium is a rare element that no ordinary medical examiner would think to look for.'

'The police specialize in extraordinary medical examiners,' I said. 'They've probably discovered something by this time.'

Wyndham didn't answer.

'And how would our murderer manage to feed his victim the necessary dose?' I asked.

'Any number of ways, only he wouldn't feed it to him.'

He was confusing me again. 'I don't get it.'

Wyndham leaned forward. 'You must let yourself go, Ericson. You've got to match your murderer's imagination. He could fix things so that his victim would breathe the poison. Fix a cigarette, for instance, with a small glass capsule full of arsine; when the heat of the burning cigarette reaches the glass, it cracks. That'll happen when the smoker's inhaling. He'd get a lung-full, and that would be the end. Or have the capsule in a handkerchief and somehow break it under his nose. Hell, anyone with brains enough to figure out the scheme in the first place would manage to get the arsine into his victim's lungs.'

'And what would be found at the autopsy?'

He thought a moment and then shook his head. 'Give it the usual time lapse — six to twelve hours — and the remaining arsenic will be practically gone. By the time the routine analyses have failed to reveal arsenic, and the examiner has become worried enough to try further checks, the unstable arsenic would be effectively gone.'

'Disappeared?'

'Not exactly. He'd have two clues, if he were clever enough to spot and understand them. The corpse would be radioactive to an unusual degree, a fact that could be determined with Geiger counters, electroscopes. Or by leaving a piece of photographic film strapped to the corpse for twenty-four hours. The other clue would be the presence of germanium — provided, as I say, he could find a way to detect it. The spectroscope might — I'm not sure. But it would take a mighty shrewd medical examiner to deduce that the presence of germanium, plus a slight radioactivity, really meant that the victim died of radioactive arsine.'

I tried to relax and force myself to retain my schoolboy expression. The questions were crowding in on my tongue. It was an effort to nod him into continuing.

'Of course,' Wyndham went on, 'you've got to realize that theory is rather more than a little farfetched. I can't believe that your man was murdered by radioactivated arsenic, because the murderer would presumably have to be a nuclear physicist.'

'Does that mean you don't believe atomic experts ever commit murder?'

'It would seem incredible to me. Murder is inherently a highly emotional business. A top-drawer nuclear man has been forced, by years of training, to approach all his problems in a logical, rather than an emotional frame of mind. It's — well, it's out of character.'

I had to laugh at that one. I said: 'I can think of a few things that might make a scientist go emotional, Wyndham. You've been reading the papers — how about the scholarly English gent who was caught selling atomic secrets to a foreign power? He must have waxed emotional at some time during his dirty business.'

'That's true,' he said, softly. 'That's quite true.'

'Then, let's put it this way: if it was done by radioactivity, one of your people might have done it?'

He let a long moment pass before he answered. 'I'm afraid I'll have to agree with you there. You can accept your conclusion as an absolute fact. No one but an active nuclear physicist connected with one of the few laboratories engaged in research, using one of the few uranium piles, could arrange to produce the radioactive arsine. It would take a full-fledged atomic pile, operating at a fairly high level.'

I let the silence build. He put down his glass and began to pace the room. He slapped his open palm against his fist. He paused near me, finally.

'But you're just guessing at this — the police haven't found anything in the autopsy?'

'The police have great brains in the medical department,' I said. 'I have an idea they've begun to nibble close to the core on this one.'

He sat down again and ran a lean hand over his brow.

I said: 'Is there any connection between radioactive arsine and undeveloped film?'

He gave a sort of explosive snort. 'Definitely. Radioactivity was first discovered when old Becquerel put a bit of film under the radioactive pitchblende ore of uranium. The gamma rays of any radioactive material will fog film — make it look just as though light had hit it. Only gamma rays will penetrate through the black paper, or thin metal cans. The gamma rays will fog wrapped film, or film inside a camera.'

I was passing third base. 'Would the stuff retain that power after it had been breathed in by the victim? Would it kill film even then?'

He sighed a deep professorial sigh. 'I wish I could tell you graphically how awesome the powers of radioactive rays are. The trouble exists in the minds of the public. People think of matter — steel, concrete — as something strong and everlastingly real. But steel isn't solid. Steel is nothing. Even dense metal like platinum, gold or tungsten is nearly pure empty space.'

'Empty space?' I asked myself.

'Put it this way: when they start to pump air out of a vacuum tube, they keep pumping for hours. Finally, they have what we call a 'hard vacuum.' There's almost nothing left in that tube. But if every atom still left actually were a solid thing, the tiny amount of gas remaining in that tube would be so heavy that the vacuum would be heavier than so much solid lead. Thus, what you think of as a dense, solid thing, just isn't a solid at all. There are a few infinitesimally minute atomic nuclei, a few very distant electron shells, and vast volumes of absolutely empty space. It gives a perfect illusion of being solid because the individual particles move about so fast. Actually, it's no more solid than a spinning bicycle wheel. You can't stick your finger through a fast-turning bicycle wheel. But light can go shining through as though the spokes weren't there at all.

'Gamma rays shine through matter in just about the same way,' he went on. 'To gamma rays, matter is just an illusion, so far as solidity goes. Just as light can shine through the wheel, gamma rays can shine through the spinning atoms of matter. They do. Of course, light shining through a bicycle wheel is reflected from each spoke and there is a little less light on the far side of the wheel than there would have been otherwise. So, gamma rays are very slightly dimmed in shining through the atom. You can never stop all the gamma rays. But if you put enough spinning atoms between you and the source of the rays, you can stop nearly all.'

'And that's why you use lead?'

Wyndham was overjoyed with my classroom question. 'Exactly! Lead has a great many individual atoms in each cubic inch, and a great many 'spokes' in each atom wheel to absorb gamma rays.' He paused again to catch a flash of understanding from me.

I said: 'I'm beginning to feel a bit smarter about radioactivity.'

'Good,' said Wyndham. 'I wish people could be told how deadly radioactivity is. They understand the bomb because it delivers a physical slap that they can see and hear in their imaginations.'

I brought him back to where I needed him. 'Suppose there were a roll of film on our victim. How would it look when developed?'

'You found film on the corpse?'

I shook my head slowly and our eyes met. He drew a blank from me. 'I'm just supposing. I'm turning scientist.'

'The film might be solid black all over, if the film had been exposed to the radiation from his body very long. It might be perfectly clear, if it were exposed for only a minute or two. But after a longer exposure to the radiation, it would be darkened in an irregular pattern, with streaks across the width of the film. In roll film, there's a metal spool which would cast a radio-opaque shadow on those sections of the film immediately behind it. If the film had been exposed in the ordinary way, in a camera, before the gamma rays got at it, there would be traces of the light-images, heavily fogged, in the areas protected by the metal spindle of the spool.'

I said: 'Would the original snapshot mean anything under all that stuff?'

He shook his head. 'Probably not.'

I finished my drink while he expanded the explanation of the dead film. When he wound it up I reached for my hat and coat and shook his hand. His grip was still warm, but less powerful now and his face looked drawn and cold.

'You've been a great help, Professor Wyndham,' I told him. 'A light in the darkness. I'll let you know if any of your statements tie in with the police evidence. It may take time — the police are being awfully cagey about what they're releasing. But I'll come up to see you just as soon as something breaks.'

'Do that,' he said. 'I'll be anxious — quite anxious to hear.'

But he didn't look anxious.

He looked worried.

19

It was very late when I rang Sybil Drake's bell.

Sybil wasn't fooling about her culinary skill. She brought me a meal of well spiced salad, cold chicken sandwiches, good beer and better coffee. She served it out of her kitchen. She was dressed in a gay and lavish pajama outfit, a scarlet creation held together by a broad crimson sash around her delightful waist.

We ate in the small dining room, a cool and restful chamber, done in quiet grays. She served on a cosy table, designed for the comfort and satisfaction of two people and no more.

After the chicken, she said: 'Now do you believe I can cook, too?'

'I'll believe anything after those sandwiches. Where did you learn to manufacture such fodder?'

'I've been around. A girl can't live on her good looks.'

'She can if she knows a good delicatessen.'

We carried our coffee cups into the living room. We sat together on the crimson couch, sipping the good brew and making smart talk.

I said, 'How is friend Dolly?'

Sybil drew away from me and made a face that wrinkled her nose.

'How can you think of Dolly at a time like this?'

'Business.'

'Before pleasure?'

I moved closer to her. I put down my coffee cup and lit a cigarette for each of us. 'Not enough business to interfere with pleasure, Sybil. I've been thinking about Dolly. After all, a man has to give a customer a little thought.'

'During off hours?'

'I've got no hours. My desk is under my hat. How well did you know Dolly in her youth?'

'A business question?'

I patted her hand. 'I'm only going to ask three.'

She thought a bit. 'I knew her pretty

well. We were together in the same show. That doesn't mean much, naturally. I didn't room with her. I just knew her as another broad on the line.'

'Did she have many boy friends?'

Sybil whistled and rolled her eyes. 'She was a female wolf, that dame was. She had plenty of guys on the make for her. They would pick her up after hours and make a play for her a while and then they would drop her. It was sort of a routine with Dolly. She never wanted to go steady with one gent, if you get what I mean. She played the field in every town we hit, all the time getting just as many jerks as she wanted. And she seemed to want plenty.'

'No one man ever got to her?'

Sybil showed me her beautiful teeth in her titillating laughter. 'What kind of a question is that to ask me? Was I there? I don't know how she handled her men — I never went out with her. All I can give you is the consensus — the way all the girls felt about her. All of us figured Dolly as strange. She had her pick of some of the best men in the field. She held on to each guy for only a little while and then moved on to the next. If you mean, was she in love, I can't answer that one. For my money she was strange, somehow.'

'But you didn't know her when she met and married her late husband?'

'I lost touch with Dolly when I left the business. I wasn't so fussy. When I found my man, I married him and stayed with him until he conked out. And he died natural, in bed, from hardening of the arteries, Spencer did.' She leaned close to me and put her hand on mine. 'Any more questions?'

I reached for her and pulled her to me and kissed her.

When she got away, she said, 'Is that another question?'

'It is, if you know the answer.'

'I should slap your face.'

'You should, but you won't.'

So I kissed her again and when we were finished I took her arm and started across the room with her.

We were close to the bedroom when the doorbell rang.

Sybil muttered an unladylike epithet.

'Now who in hell would that be at this hour of the morning?' she asked herself.

I said, 'Let it ring.'

She let it ring. It rang six times, paused, and then repeated.

In the next pause, Sybil said, 'Whoever it is won't be brushed off. I'll go.'

She crossed the room and disappeared into the hall. I heard the door open and Sybil's voice: 'Well, look who's here! What in hell is the matter now?'

A woman's voice said, 'Plenty.'

It was Dolly DePereyra. She swept into the living room, a symphony of ermine and gold. She was followed by a short man in a Chesterfield coat. He was an eye-glassed gent in evening clothes, about forty-five years old, who fussed with his tie and jerked to a stop alongside Dolly in the middle of the room.

Dolly was dressed for the opera. Her gold evening dress was long and sparkling. It shone with a million sequins and was cut low enough to show most of her chest. She was bright-eyed and jittery. She stood there turning her gold evening gloves in her long hands, over and over again. Her eyes were on fire, heavily mascaraed and snapping open and shut in a turmoil of blinking.

I said, 'How did you know I'd be up here?'

She came over to me and put her lean hands on my lapel. She pinched hard at my tweeds and gave me the full voltage of her eyes.

'I had to find you, Steve,' she said. 'I just had to. I called your place, but they didn't know where you were. I took a chance on Sybil's apartment.'

The little man avoided my eyes. He toyed with his black Borsalino.

Sybil crossed the room and pulled Dolly's hands away from me.

'I've got a good mind to slap you around, Dolly!' she stormed. 'I ought to smear you all over the place for that crack!'

Dolly said, 'I'm sorry, Sybil. I had to see him.'

'Did you have to make a party out of it? Why didn't you use the phone? And who in hell is this potato?'

The little man flushed. He was still massaging his hat when he said, 'We were out to the theatah, Dolly and I. My name is — ah — Smith. Thomas R. Smith, of Baltimore.'

Sybil snickered. 'What an odd name, I must say.'

He took a meek step my way and offered me his hand in a jerky gesture. I pumped it once and dropped it. It was wet and cold and as firm as his shifty eyes. He was dripping with small sweat beads and confusion. He fumbled back to his original spot and continued to smooth the brim of his hat.

Dolly stood close to me, close enough to hit me with the cloying sweetness of her perfumery.

I said, 'Do we spread out and make a party of this, or will you talk?'

I caught a flash of malevolence in Dolly's eyes. She directed her venom at me and then slid it off to stare at Sybil.

'Can I talk to you alone, or is my business public property?'

'You'd better spill your little routine

now,' said Sybil through her nose. 'I'm not moving.'

Dolly flounced to a soft chair, dropped her pretty figure into it and adjusted her skirt so that her legs were in focus. She lit a cigarette and relaxed under the first drag.

'I've been followed, Steve,' she said.

'Since when?'

'That's easy,' said Sybil, nodding toward Mr. Smith. 'Since Mr. Smith started to follow her.'

Mr. Smith fidgeted, but said nothing.

Dolly lost none of her composure. 'Do I keep talking, or do I stop to make way for your girl friend?'

I winked at Sybil. She turned away from me and stalked to the window. She stood there fingering the draperies.

I said, 'Start all over again. When did you know that you were being followed?'

'After the show. Mr. Smith noticed it, too, didn't you, Mr. Smith?'

Mr. Smith nodded feebly. 'After the theatah.'

'How did you notice it?' I asked him.

'It was when we were trying to get a

taxicab,' he said. 'There was this man, walking along the street behind us.'

'Behind you? How could you see him if he walked behind you?'

Dolly waved an impatient hand at her Mr. Smith. 'We saw him first when we were standing under the marquee. It was raining a little and there were no cabs so we had to stand there for a long time. Most of the other people ran down to the corner, but I didn't want to spoil my dress so I sent him — Mr. Smith — down to look for a cab. While he was gone I noticed this man in the crowd. You couldn't help noticing him because he was so fat. He — '

'Fat? How fat?'

'Good and fat.'

Mr. Smith said: 'He shoah was a fat man. Indeed he was.'

'He made me nervous, after a while,' Dolly said. 'He just stood there, leaning against the theatre door and making believe he wasn't doing anything but waiting.'

'I can just imagine,' Sybil muttered to the curtain. 'I can just see her getting nervous.'

I said, 'What then?'

'We decided not to wait for a cab. Mr. Smith came back from the corner and we began to walk and that was when we saw him start after us.'

Mr. Smith said, 'Exactly.'

'Where did you walk?'

'We went a few blocks and Mr. Smith decided we might as well go to The Typhoon Club, since it was near enough. When we got inside I saw him again, at a table in the corner, just sitting there and watching the show.'

'Did you see him talk to anybody?'

'Only the waiter. He made me nervous so we got out of there and went to another club — The Club 99. It was after I saw him in The Club 99 that I really got scared. We decided to go home then. We got a cab and when it started away from the club I noticed the fat man run out and jump into another cab and the other cab followed us.'

'You're sure of all this?'

She looked at Mr. Smith and he nodded dumbly.

'When we got started in the cab I

decided I'd better not go home alone. I was frightened. You can understand, can't you, Steve? After that business in my apartment I was plenty scared.'

'So you stopped the cab and tried to locate me?'

'We stopped at a drugstore and when we stopped the other cab stopped about a block away. I tried to get you and couldn't, so I decided to come up here on a hunch.'

'Was the fat man still behind you when you left the cab?'

She looked at Mr. Smith. He nodded his head again, sadly.

'I saw his cab stop a block away when we got out downstairs. He's probably waiting down there now until we come out.'

Dolly bounced out of her chair and ran over to me. She grabbed at my arm and her nails bit into me.

'I'm frightened, Steve, I'm scared to death. What can I do?'

I released her clutch. 'Relax. There's nothing much you can do, except go home.'

'Now?'

'Now.'

'Alone?'

'Not quite. You'll leave with your boy friend, here. He'll take you to the door and then depart.'

'I can't do that,' she moaned and leaned into me. 'Don't leave me up there alone, Steve. Please don't leave me alone.'

'Relax. You won't be bothered, I tell you. I'll go down with you, but allow you and Mr. Smith to enter the cab together. When and if the other cab follows you, I'll be right behind him. He'll never reach your apartment. If he does, I'll be with him.'

Sybil came away from the window and stood glaring at me, arms akimbo. 'I might have known this would happen.'

I said: 'I'll be back, sugar. This is business.'

She followed me into the hall. Dolly and Mr. Smith stood at the elevator, waiting for me.

Sybil said: 'What has she got that I haven't?'

'A case, sugar. She's got a good case.'

20

In the lobby, Mr. Smith began to fidget. He had put on his black Borsalino and the blackness of it brought out the pallor of his face. His hands were nervous by themselves now. He had nothing to rub, nothing to fiddle with. He was a frightened man. Somebody's father, scared to death.

He said, 'Is it absolutely — ah — necessary for me to take the lady home?'

Dolly gave him her scorn and turned away from him.

I said, 'A gentleman doesn't desert his lady fair in her hour of need.'

'It would be better if I could remain.'

'Better for whom?'

He swallowed once or twice.

'Better for me,' he said meekly. 'I'm a married man — '

Dolly shivered and moved closer to me. 'The little heel,' she muttered. 'I might have known.'

Mr. Smith reached into his coat and brought out an alligator wallet.

I said, 'Stow it away. There's no way out of this for you. It won't be tough. All you've got to do is accompany the lady to the taxi, remain inside the taxi until you reach her apartment, leave the taxi with her and wait there in the lobby for a few minutes. If anybody arrives, he will be in my company. If nobody arrives, the lady can go to her apartment alone. Is that clear?'

'And suppose the other man — the fat man comes?' asked Mr. Smith.

'He won't come. He can't come, unless he's with me.'

Mr. Smith brightened. He approached Dolly and put a hand on her elbow. 'Come along, my dear,' he said.

She shrugged off his hand with a sudden violence.

'Keep your clammy hands off me, you crumb!' she snarled and started for the door.

I stopped her.

I said, 'Not yet, Dolly, not yet. I'm leaving first. Stay where you are for a while. Give me between ten and fifteen minutes lead.' I guided her away from the door to the corner of the lobby. Mr. Smith followed us, his hat off again, his little fingers once more at work on the brim. 'Stay here, out of range of the lobby door. Don't move out of here for at least ten minutes.'

I left them that way, an elegant thrush wrapped in ermine and gold and a tired little man with empty eyes. When I walked through the lobby door he was talking to her back. Dolly was facing away from him, arms folded across her chest, head high and loaded with wrath and disgust.

I paused in the outer lobby to place my gun in a reachable pocket. I wrapped my collar around my ears, pulled down my hat and stepped outside into the night.

Outside, the street was cold and empty. I walked to the curb and put on the stock routine of a man leaving an apartment house early in the morning and wanting a cab. I looked north first, saw nothing.

Southward, a lone taxi squatted at the curbing a block away. I started for it. I walked fast, keeping my head into the wind until I came abreast of the cab.

The cabby saw me coming, leaned over to wave me away.

'I'm loaded, bub,' he said.

I went forward one step, swung open the door and bounced in. The cabby grunted, but before he could talk I was in the seat, beside the fat man, my gun pressed to his larded paunch.

I said: 'Well, I'll be damned if it isn't Goodson!'

The fat man quivered under the gun. I caught a flicker of alarm in his eyes, but he wiped it away and laughed quietly. I pressed the gun into him harder and he said: 'Hello! This is a surprise. A rather startling surprise, I might add.'

The cabby jerked his head our way: 'Are you gents gonna serve java back there, or do we roll?'

I said, 'Charming night for a walk, eh, Goodson? What say we pay this man off and stroll a bit?'

He stared at me for a long pause. He was having trouble making his eyebrows behave. He chuckled again, finally. 'As you say.' He leaned forward and made a move for his pants pocket, but my gun froze the gesture.

'This one's on me, Goodson,' I said and paid the cabby.

I stood there with my gun in his side until the taxi lost itself in the night. I prodded him downtown. He pulled his coat up around his neck as far as he was able. He shrugged and moved into a slow walk with me.

'A fine night for a stroll,' he said.

I didn't answer. I walked him four blocks and said nothing.

When we reached the gate, I steered him inside and we started down a winding path. After fifty yards we were strolling under the trees in the quiet and hush and loneliness of Central Park. The noises of the city faded, except for the occasional hum of an auto rolling through the labyrinths of the park roads. His heels made a clacking sound on the pavement, a fat footfall, slow and measured.

'Where are you taking me?' he asked.

'You've got nothing to worry about, Goodson. I should park your fat can on one of these benches. I should lay you out for surgery and spread your teeth around for the birds to nibble. But I'm not interested in mayhem tonight. We're just walking and talking, you and I.'

'So? And what are we talking about?'

'You. We're talking about you. You're too fat for a tail, Goodson. You stick out like a barrel of butter. Why were you playing tail tonight?'

Lamplight lit up the curves in his face and I saw the tic begin in his right eye, the slow wink, the slower smile. When we passed the lamp, the shadows filled his face with menace. He laughed lightly and nervously said: 'Even a fat man can admire a beautiful woman.'

'That smells, Goodson. Try again.'

'Oh, come now,' he said softly. 'You're not doubting my virility?'

'I'm doubting every little slice of you, from your flat feet to your fat brain. Why were you tailing Mrs. DePereyra?'

We were going downhill now and his breath came in short grunts and gasps. He slowed but his breath didn't. 'There was a man with the lady. I was following that man.' His voice had an evenness, a calmness that annoyed me.

I said: 'There's a dark corner in this park that's made to order for mutilation and infighting. We're walking that way, Goodson. We'll arrive there in about twenty minutes.'

'Interesting. And then?'

'My right arm,' I said. 'I'm going to slap it out of you.'

We had slowed to a crawl, but he still breathed hard. He came to a halt before a park bench. He shook his head slowly. He reached a fat hand to his forehead and began to massage.

'Do you mind — ' he whispered, 'do you mind if I sit down for a moment?'

'Keep moving.'

He rocked dizzily. He had closed his eyes and now his face was full of pain and his small mouth drawn down in a thin line.

'Please,' he asked in a whisper. 'I cannot walk any more. Not now.'

He staggered to the bench and fell into it. He leaned forward on his knees and his hat fell off and rolled incongruously until it hit a tree and remained there leaning against the trunk. His gray locks caught the lamplight and glistened silver as they blew in the breeze. I heard his breath again, this time louder and edged with a rasp.

He sat that way for a few minutes until he finally drew himself up and leaned his head against the bench. He closed his eyes and continued to breathe hard until the spell passed.

'I'm sick,' he said. 'I'm a sick man.'

'You're going to be sicker, Goodson, much sicker — unless you talk.'

He didn't open his eyes. He shook his head wearily and did things with his mouth. 'This is all very silly. Very silly, indeed. You and I can come to terms.'

'Can you walk now?'

'I think so. I can try.'

'Get up and walk.'

He got up slowly and we continued down the path. He was moving with an effort now. He was either very sick or very clever. I decided that he might be very sick. I knew that he was very clever.

After a few steps he stopped again. He wasn't smiling when he faced me.

'Look here, my good man, this is all very unnecessary. If you walk me any more I'm quite liable to collapse. I'm not well, I tell you. Why not be sensible? We could get just as far in a taxicab, couldn't we?'

'I don't like to maul fat men in taxicabs. In taxicabs there would be a witness.'

He scowled at me, but his anger didn't last. My gun found his paunch and I pushed him onward. He moved forward in a semi-drunken stagger and I saw his knees buckle and caught him before he fell.

I dragged him back to the bench and sat him down and watched him go through a carbon copy of his first attack of the heaves. This time it lasted longer and when he came out of it his face had a new flabbiness and his eyes were tired and sick.

I sat down beside him and waited for his next dialogue. It came in a whisper, a slow and fearsome mutter. 'You are a very stubborn man, my friend. Very stubborn, indeed.'

'I can be more stubborn. Why did you follow Mrs. DePereyra?'

He closed his eyes. 'She isn't important. We can come to terms.'

'You wanted something from her?'

'She hasn't got it.'

'You followed her because you thought she'd lead you to it?'

'Her escort interested me, I tell you.'

'You thought he might have what you wanted?'

He chuckled. 'Obviously.'

'You were off the beam. Mr. Smith was a pick-up. She found him in a bar or a restaurant or a night club or maybe on a street corner. He's a fugitive from the wife and kiddies down in Baltimore. He knows nothing.'

'But you. You know something.'

'I know plenty. I know, for instance, that somebody messed up Dolly DePereyra's flat looking for a piece of something that Dolly didn't have. I know, too, that either you or Gertrude Brown did that job.'

He tried to laugh, failed, coughed instead. 'Indeed? You are very clever. But you are wrong.'

'I didn't expect you to admit it. What were you searching for?'

'Something I would not expect to find in her apartment.' He brought his head up to normal and leaned my way. He pointed a hesitant finger at me. 'But you could find it, my friend. You are clever enough to get it for me.'

'I'm a busy man. I don't need any new customers.'

'Too busy to earn yourself a big fee?'

I played it his way. 'How big?'

'Five thousand dollars.'

I shook my head.

He leaned closer. 'Ten thousand dollars?'

'That's a lot of money.'

'I might even get you more.'

I chewed a knuckle and played it against my conscience, overacting so that he could read it in the gloom.

'What do I get for you?' I asked. 'And how much in advance?'

He sighed a deep and resonant sigh. He

reached into his coat and brought out his wallet. 'Here is a thousand. You'll get the other nine when you deliver the — ah — package.'

'The package?'

'A small package. Small, indeed. I'm looking for a roll of undeveloped film. This film has disappeared. It was being transported from Chicago by the late lamented Michael DePereyra. Yet, it never did arrive in New York.'

I took the bills from him and folded them neatly in my palm. I helped him to his feet and turned him back toward the park gate. We walked the distance in silence, slowly. He was breathing in great gasps again.

Outside the park we got a cab and I told the driver to take us to the International.

When we made the turn into Broadway, Goodson was hugging the corner of the seat, a fat tiger who grinned at me sleepily. His eyes were half open. His breathing seemed to bother him when he spoke. 'You must come up to my room with me,' he said. His eye winked at me.

'We'll have a drink on it, my friend. This should have happened a long time ago.'

'Wrong again,' I said. I slapped the bills into his fat hand. 'You've been consistently wrong for the past half hour, Goodson.'

He sat up sharply and stared at the bills. His face went dark and his little mouth curled into malevolence.

'You swine!' he roared. 'You filthy swine!' He repeated this choice bit of dramatics until it began to stick in his throat. He sputtered and after he sputtered he coughed and spat and his breathing was hard and loud and the rasp came again. He folded over his knees and dropped his hat. He groaned and gasped and shook his head, as though shaking might rid him of the horror in his body. He brought his head up from his knees and leaned back muttering: 'The doctor. Take me to my doctor.'

His voice was weak and old. He wasn't acting.

I tapped the driver on the shoulder.

I leaned close to the fat man's face. 'Where is your doctor, Goodson?'

There was a pause while he coaxed his voice through the impasse in his throat. 'Sutton,' he gasped. 'Doctor Sutton. Park Avenue. Eighty-Sixth.'

And then he collapsed. His eyes closed and his body went limp and his head rolled down against the window.

I tapped the driver again. 'Stop here. I'm getting out. Take this man to Doctor Sutton at Park Avenue and Eighty-Sixth.'

He pulled over to the curb and I gave him a five dollar bill and repeated my directions.

'You'd better step on it,' I told him.

'We'll make it. He ain't got far to go.'

'That's what I'm afraid of,' I said.

The cab U-turned at the corner and passed me in high gear and rolling fast.

21

After a long sleep I awoke when Mrs. Dunwoodie knocked to tell me it was late and my lunch was ready and so was Max Popper who had been waiting for me.

I found him in the dining room slapping a folded newspaper in his palm and chewing the cold end of a very small and very dead cigar.

When I sat down he opened the paper and nervously thumbed the pages. He found the page he wanted, folded back the sheet and placed the paper under his elbow.

'Guess what I read in the paper,' he said glumly.

'It's too early in my day for mental tag, Max. What gives?'

He pointed a long finger to the top of a column. His finger was under the word *Obituaries*.

'Anybody we know?' I asked.

'A good pal of yours.'

'Hiram Goodson?'

Max was surprised enough to remove the cigar stub and drop it into an ashtray. 'I'll be damned,' he said. 'How did you know?'

'I get around. Where did he die?'

Max squinted at the paper. 'He conked out in a doctor's office — a Doctor Sutton.'

'What killed him?'

'It don't say. The fat John was stiff when the cab got there.'

I finished my breakfast quickly. I said, 'It might be that we could pull a fast one, Max.'

'How fast?'

I looked at my watch. It was almost one. 'When did you get that paper?'

'A little while ago.'

'Evening edition?'

'Early evening. First.'

I tapped his shoulder and got up. 'Let's move, Max. We can do it if we move fast.'

'Do what?'

'Visit the fat boy's hotel room. If we get there before they've found out about this we might have a few minutes alone in his room. You know the boys up there?'

Max was on his feet. 'We can get in. Let's go.'

We took a cab to the International. I gave Max fifteen minutes. I waited under the east door, away from the heavy traffic. Nobody saw me.

In the lobby I hugged the center of the crowd, walking fast and aiming for the elevators. Nobody saw me.

I passed the potted palms in high, turned the corner near the cashier's desk, stepped forward into the inner lobby and interested myself in the artificial palm fronds at the far end, near the last elevator. I was gently fingering a frond when somebody tapped me on the shoulder.

It was Lund.

He gave me a friendly smile and a friendlier wink. 'You still chasing that blonde, Ericson?'

'What a fiend at deduction you are, Lund,' I said, putting a dose of the self-conscious high-school romantic in my voice. 'How did you guess it?'

'The old head,' he said, tapping it gently. 'Saw you make a play for her yesterday. Noticed the way you handled the competition. Got to hand it to you — the other guy didn't stand a chance.' He winked again and leaned toward me confidentially. 'Who was that egg, anyway?'

'Just a jerk.'

'Did she know him?'

'Know him?' I asked myself, as though I was surprised to hear it. 'Mary didn't know him. He was a street wolf — just a jerk on the make.'

Lund smiled at his cigar end. 'Don't play it so smart, Steve. That was Lester Henshaw. I know Lester. Lester don't go around making passes at dames. You know Lester, too, don't you?'

'I still say he's a street wolf.'

'Sure, he's a street wolf,' said Lund. 'But he's a reporter, too. I got an idea he was after an interview or something with that blonde. Isn't that possible?'

'Anything is possible.'

'Sure, anything's possible, like you say. So, if Henshaw only wanted an interview with the dame, why should you get so excited?'

'Did I look excited?' I asked, laughingly.

'No, not you. Five more minutes with Henshaw and you might have pulled him apart. You were cool as a cucumber, as they say.' Lund rocked slowly on his heels, regarding his cigar end with great affection. 'I wonder why Henshaw would go out on a limb for a talk with that Wyndham doll. You think maybe he smells a story?'

'Why don't you ask Henshaw?'

'Or was it something else?' Lund continued, still addressing his remarks to the cigar. 'Was it maybe more than a story, I wonder? I been thinking about it since yesterday. I been figuring maybe you and this dame don't click with me right. I mean maybe she's a customer of yours. Is that so dumb?'

It was getting late, too late for idle chatter.

'You hit it on the nose, Lund,' I told him, bashfully. 'I've got to hand it to you. I've met a lot of hotel dicks in my day, but there isn't one of them who can top you when it comes to deduction.' I put my head closer to his and strained to register companionship. 'You'll keep it quiet, of course? You won't spill? It's important that I operate in the dark for a while. Matter of fact, I'm on my way upstairs to see her right now. Important. You won't spill it around, will you, Lund?'

Lund appeared hurt and pleased and anxious to cooperate at one and the same time. 'I keep my mouth shut, Steve. You can count on me. I knew all along you were working for the doll. I could tell by the way you got rid of Henshaw.' He patted my shoulder. 'You go on about your business. Don't keep her waiting.'

'You're a regular guy,' I told him and pumped his hand and started for the elevator. 'I'll remember you when the chips are down.'

Lund was waving his hand and grinning when the elevator door blotted him out and we started up.

I got off at the fourteenth floor because I knew Lund would question the elevator boy when he made the trip down. I walked the one flight to the fifteenth and found Max in 1509. He sat on the bed. He was making a face at a small white envelope in his hand. He tapped the envelope against his palm and stared at it, stared at me and handed it to me.

I opened it. There was a sheet of blue stationery inside, a double-fold sheet that smelled faintly from perfume and the perfume was musk. The writing was in a feminine hand, graceful but hurried. The note read:

> *I've been calling you all night. I finally decided to come and leave a note because it's urgent that I see you! Please call me just as soon as you get in! I'll wait for your call!*
>
> *H.*

I tossed it to Max and he read it and scowled at it and shook his head. 'Who in hell is 'H'?'

'Helena. The Brown doll.'

'Helena Brown? I thought her name was Gertrude.'

'Her name is neither Gertrude nor

Brown. Her name is Helena. I found it on a picture from Mike DePereyra.'

Max said, 'That makes it easy. It also adds up to the works for Goodson. There's nothing in this room we can use.'

'You've been through it?'

He waved a hand around the room and I understood what he meant. It was a medium-sized room, out of the transient class, yet not quite deluxe. It was an eight dollar room, the type of place a well-to-do business man might lease as a permanent address for business reasons or for the semi-permanent sex arrangements of a minor tycoon.

The layout was simple. There was a bed, a simple maple bed, double, flanked by two simple maple end-tables. On each end-table stood a simple copper lamp, and under each lamp sat a simple copper ash tray. Two pictures hung on the walls, both reproductions of colonial scenes. There were two maple cupboards to match the bed. There was a closet, large enough for many suits, many shoes and two valises. The simplicity of the place rankled me, just as Goodson had rankled

268

me. The room was ready and waiting for the next customer. Mr. Goodson had lived in it for a long time and yet there were no traces of Mr. Goodson left in the place. Everything was simple and orderly and devoid of any clue to its former tenant.

I went to the larger cupboard. There was a comb and brush and nail file on the neat lace runner. The top drawer held underwear, socks and handkerchiefs.

Max stopped me at the second drawer. 'You won't find nothing but shirts in that one, Steve. The next one down has ties and collars and stuff like that. You won't find a scrap of paper or a line of writing in the joint. The fat John did his business outside of this room. Maybe we ought to try the Butler Trading Company.'

We left Goodson's room in a hurry. We walked down to the fourteenth floor and I knocked at Mary Wyndham's door.

She was on the way out, dressed for the street and surprised to see me.

She said, 'Fancy meeting you here, Mr. Ericson. And who's your handsome friend?'

I introduced Max and we walked to the elevator. 'Max and I thought we'd hang around the hotel this afternoon. I figured maybe you'd give me a lead to Frotti.'

'Frotti?' she frowned. 'What can you get from him?'

'Probably nothing at all. Where can I find him?'

She shrugged her elegant shoulders. 'I really can't help you with him, Steve. He's a rather eccentric character.'

In the lobby Lund awaited us. He stood opposite the elevators slapping a newspaper against his thigh. He came over to us and just stood scowling at me. High blood pressure was alive on his cheeks. He held the paper behind his back and corrugated his brows. He said, 'Guess what, boys, one of our clients has just kicked the old bucket.'

Max said, 'Honest?'

I said, 'Really, Lund? Who?'

He shifted his eyes into high gear and leveled them into mine. He smiled briefly for Mary Wyndham as he said, 'If you weren't standing here with this little lady,

I'd say you were both a pair of liars. I guess you boys didn't know that Goodson cashed in his chips this morning?'

Mary Wyndham gasped. 'Poor Mr. Goodson.'

'He's been here a long time,' said Lund. 'But you boys weren't friends of his, were you? You didn't know him well enough to take a short trip up to his room, did you?'

I looked at Max and we laughed at each other. 'Are you kidding? We just came from Miss Wyndham's room.'

'Of course,' Lund said. 'Any smart hotel dick could figure that out by just looking at you.'

We walked off and left him there. We said goodbye to Mary Wyndham in the lobby and crossed the street to the Amber Bar and stood there discussing Goodson and the note. I decided that the trail was cold at Goodson's end. I suggested following through on the Butler Trading Company.

Max said, 'That's the last lead on Goodson. You want me to go down there and fish?'

'Right away. Either Goodson or Gertrude Brown is tied to that outfit. We want to know which one and why.' I told Max I'd see him later at Mrs. Dunwoodie's and he finished his beer and left me alone at the bar.

I reached for my glass, lifted it to my face and opened my mouth to swill the rest of it when somebody slid alongside me. I half turned on my left elbow. It was Frotti.

'This is a surprise,' he said. 'You are the man from the train, are you not?'

'That I am,' I said and ordered a beer for him. 'And you, too, are the man from the train. That makes two of us, Professor Frotti.'

'Ah! You remember my name. And yet I cannot recall yours.'

'Ericson. Steve Ericson.'

'Of course. This is a coincidence, indeed!' He pulled at his beer, a long swallow. He wiped the suds away from his mustache daintily, using his index finger. 'Only a few minutes ago we were discussing you.'

'We?'

'Professor McCormack and I.'

'And why should two great scientists discuss poor little me?'

He laughed at my dialogue. He was putting on a great show of good humor loaded with hail-fellow-well-met-you-know-me-kid overtones. He had a habit of prodding me with his elbow whenever he felt hilarity coming on. I moved away from his elbow.

He said, 'You know, all scientists are members of a well-knit fraternity, Ericson. Scientific knowledge is no longer kept hidden in dark places and scientists themselves discovered a long time ago that it works for the common good when all knowledge is shared. That is the path of progress.' He giggled at the end of his line and it went flat and sour.

I said, 'Meaning what?'

I moved away from his elbow and the ensuing laughter.

'Oh, come now, Ericson. You follow me, no?'

'I'm far behind you.'

He put down his glass and grew serious suddenly. When he showed me his face it was no longer gay. The act had changed. 'You had a talk with Professor Wyndham, no?'

'I had what I thought was a private talk.'

He shook a finger at me. 'No, no. You must not say that. It would have been wrong for Professor Wyndham to consider your talk with him a secret. It would have been bad. You cannot be sure that Professor Wyndham thought your talk a confidential one?'

'At this point I can be positive that he didn't think our talk was confidential. Otherwise, how would you know about it?'

'Exactly.' His voice dropped to a whisper and he came closer to my side with his elbow. This time it was a gentle, conspiratory nudge. 'Scientists know a great many things that people — lay people — can only imagine possible. We had long ago come to many startling conclusions — among ourselves, that is. The fact that a man has been murdered through the use of radioactive arsine can only mean for us one of two things.

274

Firstly, that some one of us has utilized our knowledge to commit murder. An awful prospect.'

He stared into his beer and this time I nudged him.

'And, secondly?' I asked.

He looked up from his glass and focused his big eyes on me. 'And secondly, the more awful prospect that somehow, somebody outside our scientific fraternity has managed to secure the methods of murder that we have tried so desperately to keep secret. Do you understand the horror of this second thought?'

'They're both horrible. You suspect the latter?'

'But, of course!' He turned to face me squarely. 'You do not insinuate that you suspect one of our group? That is an impossible suspicion!'

'Why?'

He blubbered for the right words. He threw out his hands and said, 'No scientist would dare to attempt such a murder!'

'Do you know any layman who knows

enough to try his hand at it?'

He considered the question for a long moment.

'No,' he said, whispering again. 'I confess that it seems an impossible task for any layman, even an experienced one, to accomplish.'

'Which forces you to one highly scientific conclusion, eh, Professor Frotti?'

He didn't answer that one. He ordered two more beers instead and allowed himself the opportunity to pretend that he hadn't heard me.

He shook his head sadly. 'Yet, I cannot think of a scientist who would use such a means — '

'You know all the scientists in your group?'

'Not all of them, no. But quite a few.'

'How many would you say that you know intimately?'

He counted them mentally. 'Six.'

'And how long have you known them?'

He shrugged that one off. 'Not too long for some. Longer for others. For instance, I have known Professor Wyndham for five years. Yet I only met McCormack recently

— about a year ago.'

'The others, then, aren't really close to you? You know nothing about their backgrounds?'

'Very little. Very little, indeed.'

I said, 'Murder often goes pretty deep, Professor Frotti. It's sometimes built up over a period of years. How can you say which one of your friends might have a reason for murder?'

'I can't, of course,' he said to his glass. 'But you can understand that it would be difficult to imagine a scientist doing murder.'

'What makes it so tough? Would it be tough with a box?'

He looked up from his beer and stared at me incredulously.

'What kind of a box? What do you mean?'

'A lead box.'

He swallowed hard, an audible gulp that was no beer backfire. 'Do you mean that somebody has done murder with a box of radioactive material?'

'I don't know what I mean. A box full of it could kill?'

He clucked loudly and shook his head and fiddled with his mustache. 'Indeed it could. Depending on the radioactives it could be deadly, as deadly as a gun.'

'It could work through a wall?'

'No normal wall would stop hard radiation.'

'And how long would the process take?'

He rolled the beer in his glass before he answered. 'Not too long. It would depend on many things. If the concentration were powerful, it could kill — a few hours' exposure could force a breakdown in the blood cells in the course of the next few days. A hideous death.'

'It would bring on anemia?'

'Exactly.' He finished his drink hastily and pulled an old-fashioned watch out of his vest, squinted at it, shook my hand and excused himself. I watched him scamper out of the place, a squat and purposeful figure, in a hurry to get somewhere.

I caught the barman's eye with a bill and he came over.

'That character,' I asked. 'Has he ever been in this place before?'

The barman fussed with his rag and wiped his memory clean on the slick surface of the bar. 'Never seen him before a half hour ago when he came in here. Something wrong?'

I bounced a quarter on the bar and started out.

'Something or nothing at all,' I said.

22

I phoned the office of Doctor Paul Sutton and spoke to a voice full of soprano overtones and a nose full of nickels and dimes. I was asked my name and address and my reasons for wanting to see the great man.

'Migraine headaches,' I whined to the voice.

'You have been referred?'

'Doctor Nathan Diamond referred me.'

There was a pause and a murmuring on the other end. Doctor Nathan Diamond was a well-known neurologist. I had read his name a few days ago in a medical treatise published in a national weekly.

The voice purred and the oil was poured on the soprano to add a touch of warmth. 'If you will come over immediately, Doctor Sutton can arrange to see you now. But you will have to come immediately or wait until tomorrow afternoon.'

I met the voice in person twenty minutes later. She was a tall and bony nurse, of the upper bracket reception room type. She sported a British accent and a mouthful of gums and teeth. She gave me the full width of her cash-customer smile and bade me sit down. She pulled out a blue card from a mahogany file and proceeded to fill it with the odds and ends of my imagination.

Two other people sat in the big reception room. They were both women, both about the same age, both trying to read well-worn copies of *Town and Country*. When the nurse had finished with me she got up and crossed the room as though she were leading me through the Grand Canyon. She fingered a chair back tenderly and in a hushed voice instructed me to seat myself. She walked back to the little table between the two women and plucked a magazine for me. She handed me the magazine, beamed a bit, turned on her heel and disappeared through a door behind her desk.

The magazine was a catalogue of ceramics, printed on glossy paper, featuring knick-knacks and curios, all of which were represented to be antiques and any of which cost more than one hundred dollars. I flipped it back to the table and startled the two dowagers into earnest scowls of disgust, minor snortings and shruggings and an exchange of knowing looks.

I entertained myself by following the curlicue design on the wallpaper and counting the larger blobs of color. The large blobs were abstract units of color shaped to resemble nothing at all and obviously built into the wallpaper to confuse and irritate people who waited for doctors. I counted forty-five blobs and then the door opened and the nurse stood framed in it. She grinned at me and lifted a hand to beckon me inside.

She led me through a short labyrinth of corridors flanked by small rooms, each lit with a neat and somber lamp.

Doctor Paul Sutton did not greet me when I entered his room. He was focusing on the big blue index card. He was examining it with the intense concentration a surgeon gives to a mortal wound. He rubbed a small black goatee with an idle finger and sat there making faces at my record.

He was part of a stage setting. He sat in a huge leather chair, festooned with brass buttons and glistening with a well waxed glow. The room was large, almost too large to be comfortable. The walls were paneled in mahogany and the recessed bookshelves added a cloistered feeling to the decor in the way pasted books improve a window in Sloane's on Fifth Avenue. There were heavy draperies at each window, in browns and reds to promote the feeling of special talk at special prices.

For a while the nasal nurse just stood there smiling at me and awaiting the upturn of the doctor's head.

When he looked up from the card he raised an eyebrow and she faded.

He placed the index card before him on the red blotter, leaned forward on his elbows, interlocked his bony fingers, coughed gently and said: 'And now, Mr. Fuller — ?'

I said, 'My name isn't Mr. Fuller, Doctor Sutton. I had to phony up that card to get in here to talk to you. I'm here on business.'

He didn't change his position, but I saw his mind change. His square face flushed. His heavy brows came together over his long nose and he raised one eyebrow until his forehead showed the strain. He began to shake his head and I decided to take advantage of his silence.

'I've come to see you because I'm a detective, Doctor Sutton.'

He pushed himself back into his chair until he was almost lost in it. 'A detective? Whatever do you want to see me about?'

'One of your patients.'

He waved a hand at me. 'That's out. Doctors do not discuss their patients!'

'He's not a patient of yours anymore.'

'It does not matter.'

'Not even if he's a dead patient?'

He stood up, but so did I. I walked quickly to his side and put a dose of molasses into my voice.

'The patient I'm interested in mentioned you as his doctor. I assumed from this that you had treated him for some time. It's important for me to know something more about him.'

He continued to wave his hand at my dialogue. 'I am a specialist!' he snapped. 'Most of my cases are simply one-visit people. I'm not in the habit of revealing facts about my patients. I'm also not in the habit of discussing medicine with detectives. I must ask you to leave.'

I fingered my hat. 'Are you in the habit of going down to Police Headquarters for questioning, Doctor Sutton?'

He sat down again, suddenly. 'Police Headquarters?'

'It could be.'

'I do not understand.'

'You will, once they get you downtown.'

'Ridiculous!' he rallied. 'There is no reason for my going downtown! No reason whatsoever!'

'I've got a reason.'

'Then you must tell it to the police, my good man.'

'A good idea,' I said. I picked up my hat and started for the door.

He stopped me before I had made it.

He said, 'Just one moment, please.'

When I turned around he was standing before his desk, facing me.

Out of his cavernous chair, Doctor Sutton was a middle-sized man, but powerfully built. He had taken off his horn-rimmed glasses and now his eyes were small and weak.

'You must forgive me for my rudeness. I'm unused to this sort of thing, you know.' He laughed nervously. 'My last visit with the police happened many years ago. In my field one is not usually faced with such problems.'

When I came into range he motioned me to a chair and sat down alongside me, tapping his palm with his glasses and awaiting my next question. I didn't give it to him. I let him break the silence.

'Which one of my patients are you talking about?'

'Hiram Goodson.'

He sat back and thought about it for a moment. He put on his glasses and tongued his upper lip and looked very, very sad.

'A most interesting case. I suppose you know that he was dead before he got here?'

'So I read. What killed him?'

'Hypertension. Mr. Goodson died of a cerebral hemorrhage.'

'You got that from the police? From an autopsy?'

'But of course. Although I suspected the cause of his death immediately. I had been treating him for hypertension for a long time.'

'How long?'

'About ten months. Almost a year.'

'Regularly?'

He let his shoulders sag and sighed his answer. 'As regularly as I would expect from a man of his type.'

'What do you mean by that?'

'Simply that Goodson was the sort of man who enjoyed living. He would therefore only visit his doctor when his illness made itself manifest with an extreme symptom. And even then he came here unworried. He seemed more annoyed with himself than worried.'

'An extreme symptom? Would that mean that Goodson came to you when he had fainting spells?'

He nodded sagely. He sat there nodding and playing with his fingers until he had made up his mind about something. Then he got up and crossed the room to the book-lined walls. He bent to a cupboard and I saw him thumbing through another file of index cards. He found two cards and then returned.

He studied the cards and then held them up.

'Goodson's case fascinated me, for many reasons. Let me explain. On this card I have a record of his symptoms of hypertension, a serious disease in a man of his size and his habits.' He held up the other card. 'Here, however, I have another record, a record that confuses me. It seems that Goodson suffered from more than one complaint. The first — the complaint of hypertension — is a drawn-out affair. The second complaint is altogether different. It is something that Goodson never knew existed.'

'What was the second business?'

'Anemia.'

'That's the blood-cell stuff, isn't it?'

He smiled weakly. 'So it is.'

'How long did he suffer from anemia?'

'So far as I can tell, Goodson was a victim of that malady only recently. It all came to light suddenly, after I detected a few of the symptoms of anemia. At that point I took a blood test and discovered that his count was off.'

'How long ago did this happen?'

'Only a day or so ago.'

'It had hit him suddenly?'

'Inexplicably.'

'And after that, there was no checking it?'

'I couldn't be sure. Goodson's case amazed me. He died before I could complete my diagnosis, actually. Anemia must be charted. I didn't have a chance to finish with Goodson, because he died from hypertension before the chart could be completed.' He wrinkled his broad brow and worried himself for the next speech. 'You might say that I was suspicious of Goodson's symptoms. That's all.'

'Suspicious of what?'

'The cause,' he said.

'You suspected another doctor?'

He looked at me with a long, professional stare. 'I might have.'

'He would have died from the anemia if the hypertension hadn't hit him first?'

'I'm pretty sure of it.'

'How soon would he have died?'

'Very quickly, at the incredible rate his blood was changing. I would say that Goodson might have died within the month. Perhaps sooner.' He tapped his palm with his eye glasses. 'It was an amazing attack. It is very difficult to translate a doctor's amazement to a layman. It is more difficult to handle a patient when such symptoms become known. Yet — I couldn't do anything for Goodson. I couldn't be sure. I didn't want to frighten the man. I thought of having him hospitalized, so that his blood could be accurately charted. But Goodson was not the type of man to be easily bedded down. He was a big man — a strong man, and very stubborn. He was the type of patient who would refuse to consider himself seriously sick.' He lifted Goodson's cards again and stared at them glumly. 'Although I don't know that hospitalization would have saved him.'

The nurse tapped gently at the door and then the door opened and she smiled and stood there.

The doctor said: 'A few more minutes, Miss Farrell.'

When she had closed the door I thanked him for his consideration.

'I've only a few more questions, Doctor Sutton. Do you mind?'

He didn't mind.

I said, 'What caused the anemia?'

'I couldn't find out. Such attacks are comparatively rare. I asked Goodson the routine questions — general health, symptoms, exposure to X-ray, radium — '

'Radium?'

'Indeed, yes. The disease has been known to stem directly from overexposure to X-ray and radium. In both cases it happens accidentally, brought on by prolonged treatment or bad equipment in the doctor's office.'

'How can you discover the effects?'

He shook his head grimly. 'There is sometimes a type of burn on the flesh. A discoloration. A minor sunburn, in effect.'

'You found this on Goodson?'

'No, I did not. Goodson's illness only became traceable after I took the blood test. I knew at once that he was a doomed man.'

'The rays destroy through anemia? Beyond any relief?'

'He was doomed,' said Doctor Sutton. 'A doomed man.'

I pumped his hand and thanked him again as he escorted me to the door and through the door along the corridor to the reception room.

Here he paused. 'I've been a bit stupid, I suppose, not to have asked you how it was that you came to me. What I mean is that I'm confused by your questions about Goodson. He died, I'm sure, from a cerebral hemorrhage — from an attack brought about by his hypertension. He would have died — a bit later — from anemia. But why do you come to me? It isn't often that one finds a detective in a doctor's office. What kind of a case brought you here?'

'Murder.'

He took a step away from me. 'Do you mean that Goodson was involved in a murder case?'

'Better than that, Doctor Sutton. I believe Goodson himself was murdered.'

He opened the reception room door for me and when I passed the two women on the way out he was still standing at the door and his glasses were off again and his face was almost as pale as the white jacket he wore.

23

At Mrs. Dunwoodie's, Max awaited me impatiently. He was a caricature of a nervous wreck. He sat in the dim corner of the living room, his coat off and an ashtray full of dead cigarettes at his elbow.

When I entered he came alive and crossed the room. In the lamplight his face was drawn and the bags under his eyes were etched in a gray-purple. He fumbled another cigarette into his mouth and said: 'Where in hell have you been? This place's been jumping. Grand Central Station is a backhouse in Albany compared to this joint!'

I said, 'Relax, Max. One thing at a time. How did you do?'

He came over to me at the table near the bay window and eased himself into a chair. 'I drew a blank.'

'At the Butler Trading Company?'

The face he made was the face of nausea. 'The Butler Trading Company is nothing at all that I can figure.'

'Nothing at all?'

'Nothing but air.' He ran one hand through his hair nervously. 'It's a dead-end. I went down to the office of this Butler Trading Company first. It was after three o'clock when I got there. The door was locked. I knocked. I kept knocking, but there was no answer from inside. I stood around in the hall, waiting, but nobody came. So I tried to play it smart. I went down to the lobby and talked with the super, a big dumb gorilla with a face full of garlic and nothing upstairs. He didn't know a thing about the Butler Trading Company. He told me to see the real estate people — the outfit that rents the space in the building. So, naturally, I went back upstairs and waited some more.

'After a while I got tired of waiting and pulled out my keys,' Max continued. 'It was an easy in, because the office building is pretty crummy — you know, the old-fashioned kind, with a small hall and just four doors on the floor. I waited until after five in the men's room. Then I came out and used my keys. I made it on the fifth key. The place was as empty as my head.'

I stopped him there. 'No furniture?'

'Plenty of furniture, but no paper. The place was loused up, but bad. Somebody had gotten out of that office fast. They left only the desks and chairs and the filing cabinets — three of them, but all empty. It was getting dark and I was afraid to throw on any of the lights. I worked the place through, I went over it room by room. It was a total loss. I got nothing but dirty hands up there.'

I said: 'That might not mean anything. We may be able to check it later and find something.'

'Don't get humorous. I know that kind of dump like I know my own name. It was a front. What happens when you check a front? Nothing happens. You get nothing down at City Hall, because they never registered the company name down there. You get less from the people in the building because people who work a front never get friendly with anybody. You follow your leads and wind up with ulcers, galloping ulcers, like I did.' He put out his cigarette in a frenzy. 'But all this Butler Trading Company is nothing. Let me tell you about what's been cooking right here — '

'Not yet, Max. You followed through? You went down to the place near the waterfront?'

He eyed me with disdain. 'Of course I did. What I said about the uptown office of the Butler Trading outfit goes double for the cesspool near the docks. It was the same deal, but the downtown branch is dirtier.'

'I thought it was a warehouse?'

'So did I. But a warehouse can also be an empty warehouse, like this one was. Sure, there was a small office in the front, big enough and smelly enough for a family of midget rats. The door was easy. Inside I gave it plenty of time and found plenty of nothing.'

'Phone?'

'No phone.'

'But there was a phone uptown?'

Max nodded. 'That won't do us any good. The telephone company don't operate like the FBI. I tell you the Butler lead is as dead as Goodson.'

I said: 'The Goodson lead isn't as dead as his fat head. And when you mentioned the FBI you weren't talking through your ears. You know Fredericks?'

'Sam Fredericks, the federal dick?'

'The same. Give him the lead. Give him the whole background of the Butler Trading Company.'

Max stared at me with as much incredulity as he could muster. 'Are you kidding? What do I tell Fredericks?'

'Use your imagination. Give him anything that will tease him. Tell him you got a lead to the Butler Trading Company.'

'What kind of a lead?'

'Anything that will interest a Federal man. Dope, maybe. Or smuggling. It isn't important what you give him, so long as you sell him. Don't you see what Fredericks can do for us?'

'I forgot my glasses.'

'The Federal boys will smell out any angles we need, Max. Just give them their head and they'll go to town on the thing, ferret what we need and then maybe we can squeeze a crumb of help out of Fredericks later.'

'When do I do this?'

'First thing tomorrow.'

Max got up and walked away from the table. 'Now will you listen to me, maybe? What happened right here is much hotter than Abe Mann or the Butler Trading Company. What happened here — '

'Give it to me.'

'Get up,' Max said. 'Get up and take it.'

I got up. He led me upstairs to my room. He opened the door and waved me inside. He said, 'How do you like these apples?'

I stood there and laughed. My room was upchucked. My bed was in a state of upheaval that bordered on the lunatic. The sheets were wound in the blankets and the blankets were all over the floor. The mattress lay half off the springs. One pillow had been uncovered down to the feathers. There was a slit in the pillow case and the filling had been pulled out to festoon the red carpet with wisps of down.

My two valises were emptied of all the odds and ends I had not bothered to put away, a small pad of notes, two tubes of shaving cream, an old address book, a magazine and many handkerchiefs. The dresser drawers hung open. The seat cushion from my reading chair lay under the bed and even that had been slit and prodded by some anxious hand.

I walked among the debris, while Max stood in the door scowling at my discomfort.

I said, 'A pretty good job.'

'Pretty good?' he snorted. 'I'd call it perfect.'

'Where's Mrs. Dunwoodie?'

'Probably at the movies. I walked in here a half hour before you got back. I figured you were in, maybe. I figured wrong. Somebody knows how this dump operates, he had to know. He must have watched the routine in this place and walked in at just the right time for a job like this. He wouldn't have to be too smart. Mrs. Dunwoodie goes out almost every night. So do the others.'

The front door opened and somebody

came in. The somebody was Mrs. Dunwoodie. We heard her shout from the downstairs hall. 'Is that you, Maxie, dear?'

'Maxie dear is up here, Ella,' said Max, straining for an imitation of her voice. 'Maxie dear wants Ella to come up here.'

She giggled and skipped up the stairs. Max ushered her into my room and stood back to enjoy her gasp of horror. She held her little hand to her mouth and chewed the orange ends of her nails.

I said: 'Don't be alarmed, Mrs. Dunwoodie. This is all to the good. When the opposition resorts to this sort of horseplay, it means we've passed third base and are ready to slide for home.'

'I don't understand,' she whispered. 'Who could have done this? Do you think it might have been the maid? Who else? Isn't this simply awful?'

'It wasn't the maid,' Max growled.

She stared at him, round-eyed. 'It wasn't the maid?'

I said, 'Sit down, Mrs. Dunwoodie, and let's try to think this thing through.'

She looked at the bed and stepped back. 'Then let's go downstairs. Do you mind? This room just terrifies me.'

We went downstairs and sat her on the sofa. I gave her a cigarette and Max gave her a drink.

I said: 'It wasn't your maid, Mrs. Dunwoodie. All of it was planned on the outside, unless one of your boarders went berserk, suddenly.'

She assured me that her boarders, all five of them, were respectable people with good jobs who paid their rent regularly and were beyond suspicion.

Max winked at me slyly. 'How about the outside, Ella? You been making any new friends recently? Any boy friends?'

She pushed him playfully.

I said, 'A good question, Max, if you make it a general question.'

Mrs. Dunwoodie asked, 'What does that mean?'

'It means this: you might have met somebody recently. If this somebody wanted to make a play for my bedroom, it would be easy to set up his working hours. It would be easy, too, even if the stranger didn't meet you and talk to you. He might have observed you and learned the pattern of your routine.'

She shook her head slowly and blushed a bit. 'But I didn't meet anybody. Honest I didn't, Maxie.'

'How about a woman?' I asked.

She thought a bit. 'No, not even a woman. I don't have much chance to make new friends. The house takes up most of my time. And I usually go to the movies alone.'

Max walked away from her, grinning. He walked to the window and stood there surveying the street. He turned, suddenly. 'What about outside, Ella? You noticed anything outside? Anybody hanging around?'

'Hanging around?'

'In front of the house? Across the street?'

'I wouldn't know.'

'You might, if you think a bit,' I told her. She thought a bit. 'A woman, perhaps? Think of a woman, Mrs. Dunwoodie.'

Max stood over me. 'What are you getting at, Steve? You figure it was — ?'

'Gertrude Brown,' I said. 'A woman in a leopard coat.'

'How do you get there?' he asked, irritated. 'How can you be so sure?'

'I'm not sure. I'm whistling in the dark, putting one and one together.'

'One and one?'

'Goodson and Gertie, you ape,' I said. 'Goodson was after a roll of films, remember? If Goodson was searching for those films, so is our fat-hipped Gertie Brown. Goodson conked out before he got those films. That leaves big-hips.'

'How could she guess you might have them?'

'She wouldn't have to guess. Maybe fat boy Goodson was the man who knocked me silly in the train. Maybe it was Gertrude Brown. They might easily deduce that I had those films, after trying a raid at Dolly DePereyra's and not finding them there. It isn't at all tough for us to put Gertrude Brown up in my room tonight. She had been operating with Goodson, trying for those films. Goodson dies. She's left alone, to carry on the search. Obviously she might consider it shrewd to give my room a complete going-over before crossing me off her list of possibilities.'

'It could be,' said Max. 'It might have something to do with that note she left for Goodson. Maybe she decided to come up here and wanted to talk to Goodson about it before she got on her horse to louse up your room.'

I was about to say 'Now you're using your head, Max.' I didn't quite make it. The phone rang and upset my dialogue.

Mrs. Dunwoodie answered it and handed it over to me. 'It's a woman,' she said.

The voice was unfamiliar, low-pitched and urgent. The woman spoke fast and her first sentence tightened the muscles of my hand and started the sweat rolling.

It was Gertrude Brown.

24

She said, 'This is Gertrude Brown. I must see you.'

'I can't wait,' I said. 'Especially after the dry cleaning you gave my room.'

'Your room? I don't know what you're talking about.'

'You've got a bad memory.'

The tempo of her speech quickened. 'I've got to see you. Right away. Can you come over right away?'

'A jolly idea. I can't wait. I can't forget the lovely hours I spent with you, Gertrude. I'm burning up to sit on your sofa and have my head jerked around. Who have you got for me tonight, now that your fat friend is gone?'

'Please,' she whispered. 'There's nobody here. Nobody.'

If she was acting, the act was solid. Her voice vibrated with unease and trouble. The tremor came over the wires clearly. It was a perfect pitch for terror, modulated to suggest urgency and impending doom.

'I can take what you've got over the telephone, Gertie.'

In the pause, I thought I caught her breathing.

'Can I come to you?' she asked.

'You've been to me.'

'I'll come to you,' she pleaded.

'I won't be here. Spill it over the phone or put it in a pot and boil it.'

She added a throb of desperation to her voice. 'I've got something for you — something you're looking for!'

'What am I looking for?'

'You're still working for Dolly DePereyra, aren't you?'

'Maybe. Who do you work for?'

'I've got something to tell you about the DePereyra case,' she said. 'Something you need.'

'Why should you give it to me?'

'I want to give it to you.'

I laughed at her. I said, 'Your fat boy friend pulled the same gag on me, Gertrude. He was cute as a Boy Scout, but strictly out of character. He was as unbelievable as a Hollywood press agent.

I walked the legs off him in Central Park just before he died and I got the impression that he was a beaten man. For my money you're behind the eight ball now, without him. I wouldn't trust you as far as I could throw you. You play too rough for a bashful boy like me. You'll either talk fast and straight right now, or I'll hang up.'

There was no answer to my anger. There was the whisper of a sigh and then silence. My hand was tighter on the phone now and I felt the dampness spreading on my palm. The silence grew until it made me feel foolish, but I kept the phone to my ear until a faint click told me that she had given up.

I put down the phone and got my hat and coat.

Max said, 'What now?'

'We're leaving, Max. You got a gun?'

'Upstairs, I've got one.'

'Get it.'

He ran upstairs and returned with his gun. Mrs. Dunwoodie watched us leave. We ran into the street and she followed. She paused on the stone porch and just stood there fiddling with a little bow on her dress.

A yellow cab stopped for us and I gave him Gertrude Brown's address.

Max said, 'What's the gag? I thought you told her — '

'I don't play games the way she wants them played. If she's got anybody up there with her I want it to be our surprise party — not hers. She sounded worried — almost scared. I got the idea, too, that she might have something for us. After all, Goodson might have left her all alone in the swindle. If she hasn't got anybody else, we may be able to bargain with her. If she's levelling, it may be that she knows plenty about DePereyra. We're getting paid to find out things about DePereyra.'

'Nuts,' said Max. 'We're getting paid to find out who knocked him off. For my money we're still off the beam. Or do you think that Gertrude Brown knocked him off?'

'It could have been Goodson.'

'And if it wasn't?'

I shook my head because I didn't know. Max continued to annoy me. 'Then where does it get us? The way you've been acting, I figured this deal was ready to bust wide open. First it was Mrs. DePereyra and her bottle of poison. After that, you figured Goodson. And after Goodson comes Gertrude Brown. If she's got something for us it can't possibly be about herself. She's going to give you a song and dance about Mrs. DePereyra. She's got to. Who else could she talk about?'

'I don't know, but I've got ideas, Max. I have a feeling that we came into this thing at the wrong end. We've been sidetracked because we walked in through the back door instead of the front. We came into it through Dolly DePereyra, instead of her husband. We still don't know anything about him except that he was connected vaguely with Goodson and Gertrude Brown. He was carrying something from Chicago on a roll of film, but the film is meaningless because it was loused up by the radioactive arsine somebody fed poor Michael. However, neither Goodson nor Gertrude Brown knew that the film was worthless. Just before Goodson died he was actively interested in that roll of film. He was ready to pay me a roomful of rugs for the roll.'

'He could have killed DePereyra just to get that roll.'

'He could have, but he didn't.'

'How do you know?'

'I have it from the scientific authorities that no layman could have murdered with that kind of arsenic unless he knew plenty about radioactivity.'

'He could have known.'

'I doubt it.'

'He doubts it,' Max said to himself. 'The great brain doubts it.'

The cab was three blocks from Gertrude Brown's when we hit a minor traffic tangle. A cab had rammed into the fence alongside the grass plot that ran up Park Avenue. Another cab had tried to climb over it, but hadn't quite made it. We crawled along at two miles an hour.

The cab wasn't getting anywhere so we left it and walked the rest of the way to the apartment.

In the lobby, the elf on the deer was still afraid of the frog, the gloom was familiar and so was the quiet and the furniture, and the elevator man. He was the old man, heavy and gray-haired and sporting spectacles and a bad ear.

He took us up and when we got there I asked him a question. I asked him whether he had taken anybody else up within the last half hour.

He thought a bit and said: 'Five people. Mr. and Mrs. Ormsbee to the eighteenth floor. A man to the fourteenth. A man to the twenty-second. A young lady to the sixteenth.'

'Miss Brown is in?'

'Been in all night.'

'Alone?'

He wrinkled his face in a coy smile and winked at me. 'You never know, bub. You just never can tell.'

We let him go and walked down the hall and rang Gertrude Brown's bell. We heard the chimes, but nobody came to the door. I rang again and then again.

Gertrude Brown didn't answer.

Max said, 'I told you it was a gag.'

I remembered her voice and our conversation and decided to ring again. In the silence after the chimes I fingered the doorknob, pressed against it and it opened.

The hall was dark but a small light glowed from the living room. In the living room a woman's coat and hat — a leopard coat and hat — lay on the arm of the sofa. There was a handbag on a small table. It was open. It was open in a funny way. A small handkerchief hung half out of it, and beyond the handkerchief there was a lipstick, a small compact and a brown cloth change purse.

Max walked over to the table, but I waved him away. We crossed the living room into the bedroom. The bedroom was empty.

We returned to the living room and Max said, 'If she went out, she's in the building.'

I motioned him into the kitchen and we found it as spotless as it was during my last visit. We left the kitchen and walked slowly through the living room into the hall. We stood there stupidly gawking at each other and doing nothing.

Max said, 'The john. We forgot the john.'

The bathroom was located in a small hall just off the living room. I stepped forward toward the door, but Max's hand gripped my elbow and held me back momentarily. He was pointing at the floor, at the sill of the closed bathroom door. A thin rib of light lit the floor. Somebody was inside.

My arteries hardened into a lump at my throat. I heard Max whisper a word of caution over my shoulder, but it was a foolish sentiment.

I opened the door and found Gertrude Brown on the floor. She was sprawled in an awkward heap, her head thrown back against the bathtub and partially hidden by the shower curtain. Her mouth was open and her uppers showed in a macabre grin. I crossed the small rug, stepped gingerly over her legs and plucked the curtain away from her head.

She was well made-up for death. In the light, her face seemed alive. She might have fainted in that position. She might have, but she hadn't.

314

There was a hole in her head, a bloody mess smeared all over the right side of her forehead. A bullet had made that hole. Somebody had forced Gertrude Brown to walk into the bathroom and accept her doom. There were no bloodstains on the small white mat near the tub. The shower curtain held only a small blot of crimson at the spot where her head had fallen back when she fell. She had been standing on the white mat, facing the door, when the gun was fired. In the pictorial section of my imagination, the scene was pat. I could see the positions of murderer and victim. I could imagine her standing there, talking fast and with conviction, arguing for her life. I saw it all. But there was a big open gap near the door. I could not see the murderer.

Max pounded the wall over the tub and then tried the same routine over the sink.

'It was a smart pitch,' he said. 'Whoever did the job had a good head for it. Look at this room, Steve. It's practically soundproof. The way it sits, there wouldn't be much noise escaping, except by way of that little window on the street. She could have been knocked off nice and quiet.'

'Save it,' I told him. 'We're getting out of here.'

I looked at my watch. We had been in the apartment for a little over ten minutes, including the session of bell ringing. We ran through the living room and rang for the elevator.

The old man squinted at us over his glasses. 'Going so soon?'

'We never arrived, pop,' I said. 'Miss Brown isn't at home.'

'She ain't? But she must be. I didn't take her down.'

Max shrugged. 'She's probably asleep then. We've been ringing her doorbell for the last ten minutes.'

In the lobby, I added. 'When she comes down in the morning, tell her that Mr. Henry Ketchum was here to see her with Mr. Smith. Will you remember the names? Ketchum and Smith.'

'Ketchum and Smith. I'll remember 'em. They're easy.'

A sharp wind had come up from the

North and it didn't improve my chilled spine. It whipped along Park Avenue at a lively clip and added vague shiverings and mutterings to Max's dialogue. We pulled up our collars when we turned off Park Avenue toward Lexington. We got a cab at Lexington and told him to drive us home.

Max said, 'Why would anyone plug a dame that way? I can see knocking off a dame from the distance, or poisoning her, or even slugging her. But firing a gun from so close is really dirty. Who in hell do you figure would do a job like that?'

'I'm not sure,' I said, 'but I've got a few solid ideas now.'

'Now he has ideas,' Max growled to his cigarette. 'Now he's an idea man, all of a sudden.'

25

The story broke in the newspapers the next afternoon, crowding vital Washington news off the first page. It was a field day for the press boys. Nothing since the 'brutal slaying of a Long Island police man' had merited such a display. The set-up was perfect for conjecture, combined with copy that could titillate. The press treatments were loaded with overtones of sex, illicit love, a jealous lover, a jealous husband, a jealous wife, a sex maniac, a homicidal crook, a rapist, and the ever useful 'Mystery Man'.

The police threw the news boys a bone for the later editions. One of the squad men had found a picture — a picture of a man, autographed 'Michael.'

It made all the front pages. It created such headlines as:

IS MICHAEL THE MURDERER?
WHO IS MICHAEL?

DID MICHAEL KILL?

And the obvious tabloid shocker:

DO YOU KNOW THIS MAN?
HE MAY BE A MURDERER!

I wondered how long it would take the police to compare DePereyra's photograph with a close-up of his corpse. The newspaper desk sleuths were making much of the mysterious gentlemen who left their names on the night of the murder. The old elevator man had remembered the names I gave him and clung to them resolutely. Mr. Ketchum and Mr. Smith were being featured as murderers by the catch-as-catch-can school of editorial detection. The elevator man's description of Max and me was a mess of senile fabrication and bad observation. Mr. Ketchum was a tall, sinister-looking chap with a scar near his left ear and a dirty smile. Mr. Smith was even more outlandish — a short, murderous man with a pulled-down hat and a sinister eye. We had acted 'tough' and 'nasty' and seemed to be in a great hurry to leave the premises.

I was in my bedroom, chortling over the daily press, when Mrs. Dunwoodie knocked timidly and entered.

She said, 'There's a woman to see you.'

'What kind of a woman?'

'She says she's a client of yours.'

'Send her up.'

Mrs. Dunwoodie meditated on my pajamas for a second. 'You want to see her the way you are?'

'She doesn't mind pajamas.'

Mrs. Dunwoodie clucked sadly and went out. I heard her slow tread on the stairs, going down and then the more rapid patter of Dolly DePereyra's high-heeled shoes.

She burst into my room in a dramatic sweep. She carried a folded newspaper under her arm and in her hand a small lace handkerchief. She came to a halt at my bed and went through the motions of mopping an invisible tear from her eye. She handed me the newspaper and sat down near me. She lifted the silver fox cape from her delicate shoulders and let it

320

fall in a heap between her elegant legs. She was wearing a green dress, undecorated around the bosom and of a material that teased with an arresting sheen. Around and about her was the cloying aroma of her favorite perfume. She began to sob and I got off my right hip and sat up.

I said, 'What are you crying about?'

She sniffled and talked into her handkerchief. 'It's awful. That woman — and Michael's picture.'

'Why should that knock you out? You knew he was playing around.'

She looked at me over the edge of her handkerchief. There was no mist in her eye. It was the same soft eye that had attracted little Mr. Smith from Baltimore. 'I've never seen any of his — women before. This is the first time.'

'And the last, unless the others come to his funeral.'

She rubbed at her nose, gently. 'Don't be so hard-boiled. After all, he was my husband.'

'He was a heel, and you know it.'

She fumbled in her purse for a

cigarette. She found a small gold lighter and her hand was steady as she lit the cigarette. She was beginning to annoy me.

I said, 'Did you stop in just to cry on my shoulder, or was there something else you had in mind?'

'Don't be angry with me. I was really sick when I saw Michael's picture in the paper. I haven't any friends to sympathize with me — nobody to share my troubles.'

'What happened to the big man from Baltimore?'

She didn't answer. She leaned back on her hands, far back on the bed. She took a deep drag and held her face deadpan.

'You don't have to be so tough and mean, do you?' she asked.

The mid-afternoon sun crept through the draperies and lit the edge of my bed. In the fresh light, Dolly's make-up was edged with a theatrical shine. There was too much color on her cheeks and the mascara held a purplish glow. In the sunlight, her lips brightened to an artificial crimson, the type of color they build into subway posters. The green of her dress threw her face into awful contrast. Her chest rose and fell in a quickened rhythm. For a long minute I felt uncomfortable in my pajamas.

'Get to it,' I said. 'What do you want?'

'Must we hurry?'

'Either you hurry or I walk out and leave you alone with your imagination.'

She sat up and made eyes at me. 'You are tough, at that.'

'I can be tougher.'

'You don't like me.'

'It's too early in the day for horseplay. What's bothering you other than my pajamas?'

Her eyes went cold, but it was a fleeting freeze. They melted immediately and she stood up and came over to me.

'I only wanted to talk to you, honestly.'

'Do you think you can make it, or should I get dressed?'

'I only wanted to discuss how the case has been coming.'

'I'm almost finished with your case,' I said. 'I'll tell you all about it. Later.'

'You mean you know who killed Michael?' She seemed enthusiastic. She was almost gay.

'Pull yourself together and go down-stairs. I'm going to get dressed now. I'll be with you in about ten minutes and I'll tell you all about it.'

She picked up her fox and threw it over her shoulder with a well-practiced gesture. She tipped her cigarette on the rug and walked past me slowly. I opened the door for her and she went out.

'Take your time,' she said. 'I don't mind waiting.'

I dressed quickly and when I reached the living room she was smeared on the sofa in a soft pose. She had arranged her skirts so that the curves of her legs were featured. Mrs. Dunwoodie sat near her, playing hostess. Mrs. Dunwoodie caught the message in my eyes, got up and left us together.

I looked at my watch. It was four o'clock.

I said, 'We've got just about thirty minutes for smart talk. You came here to hear about the case and here it is. I thought I was close to your husband's murderer. I thought I had him two days ago. I don't know yet whether I was right or wrong. I may never know, because the man I suspected has died.'

She gasped. 'Died? Who was he?'

'What difference does it make to you? You couldn't have known him. You've told me more than once that you knew none of your husband's friends.'

'He was one of Michael's friends?'

'He might have been. He might have been a business acquaintance.'

She tried to frown but the muscles in that department didn't bear up under the strain. Her face remained deadpan. 'I don't understand.'

'That's fine. I didn't think you'd understand. Now I can follow through to the woman in today's paper. Her name was Gertrude Brown. Gertrude Brown was very close to the man I suspected. After he died, Gertrude Brown was left all alone in whatever game they were playing.'

'Game?'

'It was a game, or a swindle, or a maneuver, or a business. I don't really know. I can assume that Gertrude Brown and your husband and the other man were well known to each other. Look at it this way: your husband was a good friend of Gertrude Brown. Gertrude Brown and the other man were good friends. Therefore, we can assume that your husband might have been a friend to both of these. Your husband might have thus been engaged in some sort of a business venture with Gertrude Brown and the other man. Is that clear?'

'Not quite,' she said. 'Michael certainly knew the girl. His picture in her place more or less proves that. But I didn't see what that has to do with the dead man — the man you suspected.'

'You may be right, but we'll never know. We have only a few crumbs of evidence against the dead man. He was on the train with you and your husband when you came in from Chicago. It could be that Gertrude Brown travelled with him. If they were on that train, they came in with your husband for a purpose. If the man I suspected was on the train, he had a good reason for being on it.'

'And the girl? Gertrude Brown?'

'Forget about her. Let's assume that

she wasn't on the train. I'm almost positive that she wasn't. Let's follow through on the man — the man who might have killed Michael.'

'Who was he?'

I walked over to her and looked tough. 'That's the second time you've asked the same question. Would it really make you happy to know?'

'I'd like to know.'

'He was the fat man!'

'The fat man?' she asked herself. 'You mean the one — '

'Yes, the man who followed you and your gladiator from Baltimore. Are you happy now? Did you know that fat man?'

She was profoundly shocked. She abandoned her pose and sat up, stiffly. 'Of course I didn't know him.'

'Of course. I didn't think you knew him, any more than you knew Gertrude Brown, or anybody else connected with the case.'

'There are others?'

'There must be others. Unless the fat man killed your husband and then got up in his shroud to kill Gertrude Brown, there must be others. Somebody killed Gertrude Brown. That somebody was close to the whole mess — it wasn't an accidental death, or a maniacal burglar, or an escaped lunatic. It happened too soon after the fat man's death to be meaningless. It's been giving me ideas — changing my mind about things. A little while before Gertrude Brown was shot she phoned me. She wanted to talk to me and I didn't give her a break. It might have saved a lot of trouble. She might have been levelling.'

Dolly DePereyra studied her finger-nails. 'It's all very confusing. I wish I could help you. But I can't — all these people were strangers to me.'

'Naturally. And, of course, you had nothing to do with any part of all this?'

'What do you mean?'

'You know what I mean. You're not lily-white. You're the fond little wife who carried a bottle of arsenic in her valise, remember?'

The color of embarrassment filtered through her high make-up.

'You didn't believe me when I told you

I didn't poison Michael?'

'I still believe you. But we've come a long way from that bottle of poison, you and I. You're an unpredictable character.'

'Is that bad?' she asked, archly.

'It's not good. I don't really know you. I can't account for your behavior. I'm a detective, not a psychoanalyst. I don't understand jerks like your Baltimore beau. You make it tough for me to keep you in the clear on this whole business. You make it necessary for me to ask you where you were last night.'

'Are you asking?'

'I'm asking.'

She kept her eyes away from me, like a coy school-girl on her first date. 'You won't like me if I tell you.'

'Am I supposed to like you?'

'I'd rather have it that way.'

'You can't have it,' I said. 'Where were you last night?'

'I was out with him again.'

I wanted to laugh, but couldn't risk it. 'You mean with the little jitterbug from Baltimore?'

'That's right.'

'Where did you go?'

'We went to a show and then to the Silver Spoon. We stayed at the Silver Spoon until after three.'

'And then?'

She brought her eyes back and tried to look pure and honest. 'Then he took me home. That's all.'

'Why do you see him?'

She fumbled for a line. 'I'm lonely.'

'You picked him up?'

'Don't be too mean to me. He picked me up.'

'You never knew him before then?'

'I still don't know him,' she said with a sigh. 'I guess you'll never believe me, but I only wanted company. He's good company.'

There was a stir at the door and I heard it open and when I turned around Max was standing in the doorway appraising the scene in the living room with a dour eye.

Dolly DePereyra got up. She said, 'Can I have just a few more minutes with you — alone?'

Max turned on his heel and went

upstairs. She came over to me and put a hand on my lapel tenderly. When she spoke she put everything she had into her dialogue and brought her body close enough so that I could feel it without touching it with my hands.

'Do you still hate me?' she asked.

'I can live without you. But I'll get along with you until you pay me your fee.'

'When will I see you?'

'When it's time to pay off.'

I stepped back and away from her and walked into the hall. She followed me silently and when I opened the door for her she didn't say a word but her eyes told me that she hadn't yet given up. I wondered what a good psychiatrist would do with a woman like Dolly DePereyra. I watched her go down the steps and pause on the sidewalk to turn and give me another of her loaded smiles. Then she adjusted the fur cape and went away.

When I turned away from the door Max was standing at the foot of the stairs whistling a tune and contemplating a piece of nothing at all on the ceiling.

I said, 'You've got a dirty mind, Max.'

26

I got my hat and coat and took Max with me. I was filled with a sudden drive, the tightness that comes with the smell of theoretical success. There were things to do. It was almost five o'clock, a bad hour for visiting working citizens in a big city.

In the cab, Max told me of his talk with Sam Fredericks.

'They had that Butler dump under what they call scrutiny, for a long time, Steve. Sam explained about why they did it. He said they always check on all outfits like that — when they do business with other countries. They've got plenty on the jerk who ran the place. But the jerk just disappeared. He was a foreign agent. A spy type.'

'They've got no name?'

'Sure, the name is all they've got. Butler was the name.'

'It could have been Goodson,' I said.

'Did he tell you what the jerk looked like?'

'Do I look as dumb as you make me out?' Max sneered. 'Naturally, I asked him whether it was a fat man. The answer is no.'

'Did you ask him whether he checked the missing gent with Michael DePereyra's picture?'

'He didn't want to talk about his business too much.'

'But you suggested DePereyra?'

'Sure I did. And when I did he buttoned his lip. I got the idea that maybe he knew more about DePereyra than he was telling.'

'It could fit that way,' I said. 'It could fit tight and solid.'

Max leaned forward and examined my expression carefully. He was in character, sour and cynical, when he asked: 'What have you got that I don't know?'

'I've got the pitch. It's simple, if you begin at the right end. DePereyra, Goodson and Gertrude Brown were in business together. They were playing for big stakes. But they were playing a dirty game. They were blackmailers.'

'All three?'

'All three,' I nodded. 'We've got them tied together by simple evidence — the notes in DePereyra's wallet, the telegram and the fact that Goodson was so chummy with Gertie Brown — DePereyra's girl friend. The next step is to figure their racket. I say it was blackmail because Goodson was hell bent on finding a roll of films. He was ready to pay off handsomely for these films because they were the stake in the blackmail. Do you follow me?'

Max was on his toes. 'You mean that he wasn't using the films to blackmail with. You figure just the opposite; that he was blackmailing to get those films?'

'Exactly. And that brings us to our problem — to find who Goodson and DePereyra were blackmailing. If we find their victim, we've got the murderer.'

'Worse and more of it,' moaned Max. 'How do you figure narrowing down the hunt?'

'It's all figured for us.'

'You know more?'

'Plenty. But what I know you'll know soon.'

'You finished?'

'I'm winding it up. Today.'

'How?'

'The old tease,' I said. 'We're going to pull a fast one.'

'Who's the customer?'

'If I knew for sure, I wouldn't be playing games. We've got plenty of customers to fiddle with.'

'We're going to suck them in?'

'We're going to try.'

The cab stopped before the Courier Building. We took the elevator up to the city room. In the reception room, Max said: 'What am I doing?'

'Ask the girl for Lester Henshaw.'

'Why do I want to see him?'

'Because he won't see me. Tell him you've got a break on a big story. Tell him anything that sounds dirty, but get in to see him. I'll be right behind you.'

Max told the receptionist his story. There was a short pause while she made contact with Henshaw. I saw her mouth move in the stock questions a receptionist must ask a strange character. She put down the phone and waved him inside. I caught him as he swept into the clatter of the city room and gave him a lead toward Henshaw's desk.

Henshaw didn't see me until Max had begun to talk. He got up from his desk and began to splutter righteous indignation.

I said, 'Relax, Lester. I came up to apologize.'

'The hell you did.' He disregarded the hand I held out to him. He surveyed me with apprehension and distaste. 'I've got a good mind to have you kicked out of here, Ericson.'

'You've got a good mind only if you let me stay. I've got something for you.'

'You know what you can do with it.'

Max turned to me with a bitter taste on his face. 'Do we have to take this kind of crap from him? Let's get out of here — he turns my stomach.'

I walked around the desk and when I reached Lester's end he had backed away from me. I sat down in the chair near his.

I said, 'You wanted the wind-up on the

DePereyra case, didn't you? You wanted a story? I've got one for you.'

For a moment he struggled with his newspaperman's conscience. It was a losing battle. 'Why should you do me a favor?' he asked.

'Because you can return it.'

Lester came closer. 'Double-talk. What are you getting at?'

'Sit down and rest your head, Lester. We can do business.'

He sat down. 'I'll do business. But I warn you that I haven't forgotten what happened between us. I'll make you no promises. I'll listen and tell you later.'

'You'll make promises. I've got the wind-up on a combination of newsbreaks that will rock the country. I've got murder and big names and a cast of characters that will boost Henshaw from *The Courier* to *The Times*. I've got dynamite. But there's a pitch, Lester. I've got a few questions for you to answer first.'

The struggle was over. He had jerked out his pencil and placed a sheaf of yellow sheets on his desk during my dialogue.

'I gather that you're about to ask me

for my right arm,' he said. 'What's the pitch?'

'Background. You were up at the International, nosing around a blonde for a story. Why?'

'She's good copy. You can understand why.'

'What were you digging up there?'

'I was just browsing. That convention is loaded with good newsprint if a man can whip up an angle. I was trying to interest the Wyndham dame in an interview. She's good for a barrel of words and from what I saw of her legs there would be good cheesecake to go with it.'

'Is that all?'

'Would you believe me if I said yes?'

'Maybe I'll have to believe you, Lester. Did you try any of the others up there?'

He pulled out a small notebook and flipped the pages. He stopped in the middle of the book and pushed it before me and pointed to his spider-web scrawlings. 'Read that. There are my notes, my reasons for trying for a story up there.'

He was telling the truth. The notes

were brief, but promoted the idea of researching among the atomic bigwigs for a lead to a series of interviews. I saw the name Oscar Wyndham at the top of his list.

'You spoke to Oscar Wyndham?'

'Wyndham is not new to me. I met him years ago when he was on a lecture tour in the East. He promised to give me a bit of time just as soon as the conference was organized. After him, I tried his niece. That was all.' He stopped tapping his pencil and said: 'I'm giving you this straight, Ericson. What are you giving me?'

'Plenty. It's good for our side that you know Oscar Wyndham. He's the man I need. You can get to him immediately?'

'I can try, but you've still got to sell me. I'm not just going up there again for a brushoff.'

'You won't get the brush. I can guarantee that Wyndham will be more than anxious to make talk with you. We've got a tricky piece of business to finish, Lester. I'm sure Wyndham will want to be in on it.'

Lester was tapping again, impatiently. 'What do I get out of all this?'

'The works. You'll get the answer to the murder of the man on the train, plus one other murder and one semi-murder.'

He held me there. 'Semi-murder?'

'Don't make me explain it now — you'll have it all later. Here's my plan — '

'How about the police?' Henshaw interrupted. 'You mean to tell me they're not close to this?'

Max leaned on the desk and scowled. 'Why don't you let him finish, Henshaw. For my sake. I'm supposed to be his partner and I know as much as you do about the stinking mess.'

When Lester relaxed, I began my explanation.

'You will make an appointment with Oscar Wyndham. Wyndham is perfect for our scheme. He has a habit of spilling anything that smells of the scientific to his brothers in the trade. This is exactly what I want from him. When you make the appointment you'll tell him that you have it from an eminent detective, or the homicide squad, or on good authority, that the solution of many recent murders in the city is reaching a climax. At that point he will undoubtedly ask you which murders you are talking about. You'll tell him that you're referring to the murder of Michael DePereyra, the murder of Hiram Goodson and the murder of Gertrude Brown. He may not be interested in this startling news. Pay no attention to his state of mind. Work on him until he is interested.'

Henshaw stopped me there. 'Work on him? How?'

'I'm getting to that. You must promote the idea that your informant knows pretty surely that at least two of the deaths were brought about by the use of radioactivity.'

He dropped his pencil. 'Are you serious? If that's true, it's a newsman's nightmare!'

'It's true. Don't interrupt; I want you to get a clear picture of my plan.' I saw Max leave the desk, stroll a few steps and return with a dead pan alive with curiosity. 'Sit down, Max,' I told him. 'I've got room for you, too, in this thing.'

'Your job is to arouse Wyndham's curiosity, Lester. After you've got him on the hook, you'll break the topper to him. Your friend, the detective, claims that he has an important and damning piece of evidence.'

'Do I mention your name?' Henshaw asked.

'I want you to be very certain to mention my name — at the proper moment. Tell him that you've seen this evidence — a roll of film, a series of negatives on which somebody photographed important and highly secret data on the hydrogen bomb.'

Henshaw registered the maximum in surprise. He closed his fist over the pencil and leaned close to me — close enough to grab at my sleeve with his free hand. 'You've got these films?'

'I've got them. Be sure to tell Wyndham I carry them around with me, at all times. They're too valuable to leave anywhere!'

'And you know who shot them?'

'Don't be idiotic, Lester. If I were sure who did those pictures I wouldn't need you, would I? We've got a whole hotel full of suspects — a convention of atomic brainpower. I've met only some of them. But I suspect the whole crew. I'm forcing the hand of the murderer this way, don't you get it?'

'I didn't, but I do now,' said Lester quietly. 'But you're leaving yourself wide open, aren't you? You're liable to get — '

Max got up. 'I don't think so, Henshaw. Now I know what you wanted me for, Steve.'

I said, 'Is it all clear now?'

Henshaw mopped his brow. 'My job is easy. But where will I find you?'

'I'll get in touch with you just as soon as we're ready for the finish. You have my word on that. From your end, you've got to promise to keep your big mouth shut and operate the way I've instructed you. Remember, one leak on this thing and it won't come off. You've got to play the dumb reporter friend of a dumb detective.'

Henshaw shook my hand. 'You can count on me, Steve. I want the rest of this story.'

'You'll get it,' I said. 'Make your phone

call as soon as we leave.'

He was picking up his telephone when we arrived at the door to the reception room.

In the street, Max said, 'I think I know the routine from here on out. You want to go back to Mrs. Dunwoodie's?'

'Smart boy.'

'You wait there for about an hour and then leave the house?'

I whacked his shoulder. 'What a brain!'

'And after you leave the house, you expect to be followed by somebody?'

'You're getting smarter by the minute, Max.'

Max grunted. 'And after that, murderer follows Ericson and Maxie tails both of you?'

I nodded. 'Maxie makes sure Maxie is not seen by murderer. Maxie hangs back until detective needs him.'

Max shivered and said nothing.

27

It was a nice night for walking; a brisk night, a sharp night, the air frosted with the sort of cold that can even kill the dirt smell of a big town.

For no reason at all I was wandering along 46th Street. It was after nine. Between Sixth and Fifth, the street was a darkening canyon peopled only by accidental wanderers who walked quickly and earnestly toward the lights of the avenues.

The sidewalk was lined with cars, abandoned an hour ago by theatre-goers. A lone cop came flatfooting it along the pavement, setting up a hollow beat with his hard heels. He was an overgrown Boy Scout who played games with his nightstick and whistled an Irish chanty to brace himself against the sudden loneliness.

I joined him in the tune. Somewhere behind me, among the thousands of casual pedestrians, one person walked with a purpose. That person was following me, moving behind me with stealth and cunning, waiting for the pause in my walk that might give him his chance.

I passed the cop and ahead of me the lights of Fifth Avenue sparkled at the end of the bleak corridor that was 46th Street. A flow of noisy cabs punctured the gloom, raced for the lights ahead, squealed to a stop, hesitated to snort automotive impatience, and then rushed on.

I had almost reached Fifth Avenue when I felt the cab roll up behind me. I felt it because I heard it. The noise of it was behind me, a dull hum of tires on concrete; a slow roll for a taxi. And then it was alongside and the brakes squealed slightly and when I turned it had stopped and I heard a voice call my name.

It was a woman's voice, Mary Wyndham's, and it was more whisper than voice.

'Steve!'

I opened the door and stood there with my foot on the running board.

I said, 'Hello, Mary. This is a surprise.'

She slid across the seat and the lamplight showed me that her eyes were bright with fear. 'Steve, you must help me! I've got to talk to you!' She put a hand on mine and it was trembling.

I climbed aboard and she sat close to me. I said, 'You look as though you've been picnicking in a graveyard. Where do we talk? Your place?'

'Oh, no! Not there. I can't go there.'

The cabby half turned his head. 'You two want me to rent you the cab and go to a movie, maybe?'

'Drive to the park,' Mary said. 'I must see you alone, Steve. We can't be near the hotel. It would be bad.'

The cab turned up Fifth Avenue at a good speed.

'Bad? Why would it be bad?' I asked.

She was trembling again. She had pulled out a handkerchief and was trying to kill her sobs. I let her try for composure. I patted her free hand and spoke gentle words and after a while we were at Central Park. I stopped the cab on the middle road and we walked down the deserted path. She clung to me as she

347

walked and sobbed her heart out into her handkerchief.

We were deep inside the park before she quieted down. We were in a lonely spot near a giant rock and the wind blew an odd song through the filigreed branches. She sat close to me and I put my arm around her and held her there.

I held her tightly and said: 'Take it easy, sugar. Tell me what's bothering you.'

From somewhere far away a branch snapped in the wind. She shivered and then the tremor passed. 'Steve, will you give me those films?'

'Who wants them?'

'Uncle Oscar. You must give them to me.'

'Why does he want them?'

She looked up at me. 'He's in trouble, desperate trouble.'

'And the negatives would help him? How?'

'He could destroy them.'

I patted her gently. 'What makes you think I've got them?'

She raised her head and stared at me. 'Uncle Oscar told me you had them.'

'And why didn't he come for them?'

She looked away. 'He's upset, terribly upset.'

'Your uncle is an amazing man,' I said. 'He didn't tell you why he wants those films?'

'He's had a breakdown,' she said, and grabbed my hands in a burst of emotion. 'I left him at the hotel, in his room. I gave him a sedative to put him asleep. He was going through some kind of hell, Steve.'

'A normal reaction to murder.'

She dropped my hands and drew away from me. She began to sob again, but I quieted her quickly.

I said, 'He was being blackmailed by DePereyra and Goodson. They had forced him to give them photographs of highly secret research. He held out as long as he could, but they must have threatened to expose some part of his past unless they got the pictures. He decided to give them what they wanted, finally. But his conscience wouldn't allow him to follow through. He murdered DePereyra with radioactive arsine. Then he used the box on Goodson.' I dropped my voice and allowed her to consume the full meaning of my dialogue. 'I can't believe, somehow, that he took money from them. He doesn't seem the type. He's a simple man. What would he do with dirty money?'

She didn't answer.

I reached into my pocket and took out an envelope. She smiled a weak smile when I handed it to her. She stuffed it tremblingly into her handbag.

I said, 'A woman would have more use for dirty money, don't you think?'

'What do you mean?'

'A young woman could have a fine time with a jerk like DePereyra, if she had the stomach for him and the mind for his money.'

She laughed nervously. 'You're talking in riddles.'

'And you're answering in double-talk,' I said. 'Those films won't help you any, sugar. They're dead. They're as dead as Gertie Brown!'

She brought up her head and when it was on a level with mine I saw the flash of her teeth, vaguely. She was smiling, but it wasn't an honest smile. I knew it wasn't honest because something hard hit my chest, suddenly. It was a gun.

She pressed the gun into my chest and said, 'Sucker!' and then she was out of my hands and standing over me with the little automatic aimed at a spot between my eyes.

I said, 'Fancy as hell, beautiful. But I didn't think you'd have guts enough to kill me here.'

'You fool!' she laughed. 'What did you think I brought you out here for — the fresh air? You're smart, you're very clever, you had me all figured right along, didn't you?'

'You cut your own throat. You over-dressed, sugar. Research assistants don't usually buy on Madison Avenue. DePereyra must have paid off well. But didn't it ever occur to you that he was paying for information so that he could someday blast you off the face of the earth? Only a traitorous broad would have done what you did. You ought to be ashamed.'

That reached her. Her hand shook and her voice matched the tremor in her fingers. 'I'm not ashamed.'

I started for her. The sweat was rising under my hatband and I wanted to slap her around. She bit at her lower lip and stepped backward on the grass. She lifted the gun slowly and waved it at me.

'I'm going to kill you now, Detective,' she said. 'I'm going to shoot.'

I walked toward her and when I hit the grass she had raised the gun to the right height for my eyebrows. She stood there, a menacing silhouette against a dull sky, and suddenly somebody was behind her, a quick shadow that leaped at her and knocked the gun from her hand. It was Max.

I picked up her gun and we walked her through the curved lane that brought up to Fifth Avenue. We took a cab and delivered her to Police Headquarters. She didn't speak to us all the way down. And I was in no mood for conversation.

* * *

Mrs. Dunwoodie had the coffee pot heated when we arrived. She sat us down at the small table in the bay window. Max allowed me to finish my first cup and light my first cigarette.

Then he said, 'I don't get it. When I jumped for that dame, I felt like a heel. She didn't look like the killer type of doll to me. It was like jumping at my own sister.'

'She had a double-dealing brain, Max. She was the scheming sort of killer. She worked far ahead, planned carefully and almost got away with it.'

'How did you figure her?'

'I didn't for a long time. DePereyra might have been killed by any number of people on that train. There were a load of scientists — and it had to be one of them — it had to be somebody with a knowledge of radioactivity. This meant that Wyndham, Frotti and McCormack were immediately on my list. But we went off on a tangent when Goodson and Gertrude Brown entered the operations. Who were they? Why was Gertrude Brown down at the train? Was Goodson a friend of DePereyra's? These were some of the questions that drove me nuts. And we didn't get very far with either of them until Goodson died. That was the beginning of the end for Mary Wyndham.'

'She killed Goodson, too?'

'She had him fixed, anyway. He would have died from anemia, if he hadn't died of the brain hemorrhage. But the deal becomes confusing if we begin with Goodson. If you want the continuity, you've got to start with Michael DePereyra.'

Max scowled. 'That's really working it backwards. We still don't know much about DePereyra — if we know anything at all.'

'We'll know more as soon as the FBI gents hear my story. At any rate, it all started with DePereyra. He was a man without a trade. It isn't any wonder that his wife never knew anything about what he did. He made it his business to keep it from her. We do know, though, that the Butler Trading Company wasn't legitimate. It disappeared suddenly. Fredericks said it might be a front for a group of foreign agents who were out to ferret information. And what would foreign agents be ferreting this season?'

'Don't let me guess. I can't.'

'You could if you tried,' I said. 'What's in the news these days, Max?'

Max tried, and made it. 'Hydrogen bomb stuff — naturally!'

'On the nose. That's the foundation of all of the plot. DePereyra must have been assigned to the Manhattan Project. The word 'Island' in the telegram referred to 'Manhattan.' He picked Mary Wyndham because he was the type to make time through the ladies. I figure he paid her well during their phony romance, and then threatened to expose her unless she got him the information that he wanted. She took dough from him for a long time. She must have found out about Gertrude Brown and decided to give DePereyra nothing at all. She was a jealous bitch. She figured she'd murder him on the train, retrieve the film and then take care of Goodson and Gertrude Brown.'

'So she bumped off DePereyra in the train?'

'She used the radioactive arsine on him, but didn't have time to take the roll of films out of his pocket. When I got to the room she made an effort to get those films. She must have been wearing pajamas. That's why Frotti thought he saw a man.'

Max stopped me there. 'I don't get the pitch for Goodson. How does he fit?'

'Goodson and Gertrude Brown and DePereyra were all in on the scheme. When DePereyra died on the train it then became Goodson's job to follow through and get those films. His first operation was to rifle Dolly DePereyra's apartment. That job failed. He found nothing. He next tried to tail Mrs. DePereyra, hoping that she'd lead him to something. I stopped that one, and when I took him up to the park he was desperate enough to try to win me over to his side. Any kind of atomic secret is worth a lot of money to a few choice people.'

I filled my coffee cup and lit another cigarette. 'Goodson was put out of the way by a cerebral hemorrhage, but he would have died from anemia in a week or so anyhow.'

'Anemia? Is that murder?'

'We'll get to that later. Let's follow through on the spy plot. When we visited Goodson's room, we found a note from Gertrude Brown. She was probably getting cold on the deal and wanted to call it off. She never had the chance. Mary Wyndham must have contacted her that night to offer her the films. Gertrude Brown didn't want to be alone with Mary. That was probably why she called me. She was scared. She had good reason for her fright, as we saw in the bathroom.'

'The Wyndham dame killed her because she was the last one left to blackmail her?'

'Exactly,' I said. 'After that, Mary's job was done. There was nobody left alive to threaten her — except the man with the films. For that reason, I told Henshaw to contact Oscar Wyndham. Oscar had already shown us that he had an open mouth to his colleagues. I knew that he would inform all of his friends about the startling information Henshaw gave him. He would also inform Mary, because she was considered one of them. But it was at that point that Mary made her big mistake. She wasn't absolutely sure that the arsine had killed those films. She couldn't afford to have those films around, because they would prove to the police that DePereyra had been butchered by radioactive arsine. The films bothered her. They were the only small thread of evidence against her plot.'

Max whistled. 'When did you get the lead to the Wyndham dame?'

'After I spoke to my friend Lund. He told me that Oscar Wyndham had missed a powerful box of something one night. Wyndham was very much worried about this box, and yet he discovered it in his closet the next morning. Mary Wyndham was the only person who could walk in and out of his room without being suspected of pilfering. She took that box and used it that night. She set it on her bed and aimed it up at Goodson. The stuff is powerful. The rays from the radioactive stuff in the box went through the ceiling into Goodson. Goodson knew nothing — he slept through the night and awoke a walking corpse.'

'It killed him by giving him anemia?'

'Radiation out of that box was as deadly as a gun. Mary Wyndham knew that if she rented the room beneath Goodson, she could sooner or later kill him in his sleep.'

'What a woman!' sighed Max. 'She had me fooled, all right. She's going to look awful pretty in court. It'll take a hard-boiled jury to give her the works.'

I got up and went to the telephone. 'She'll get the works. The jury is going to be terrified by the idea of atomic murder,' I said and dialed Sybil Drake's number.

Sybil was cold and disinterested.

'The case is closed,' I told her. 'We've got nothing to worry about. You can cook me that steak and get the red sofa ready, sugar.'

'You're always thinking of something to eat.'

'Not always. I have my moments.'

'Can I depend on that?'

'Give me one more chance. I'll be up in an hour for a test run. Is that soon enough for you?'

'I can't wait,' she laughed. 'How do you like your steak?'

'We'll get to that later,' I said.

I started upstairs for a quick shower. When I passed Max he was whistling an old lascivious tune and examining his fingernails with great care.

'You've got an evil mind,' I told him. 'A very dirty brain.'

'I was thinking about Dolly DePereyra, our client,' said Max. 'I was wondering who gets to collect our fee from her.'

'You think you can handle her?'

'I like mental cases.'

'You can have her.'

Max jumped up from his chair and skipped across the room.

We walked upstairs whistling an off-beat duet.